Hatchet Harry

© Drew Alina 2019

To Joyce with amusement

EARLY DAYS

I was born on 30 June 1961, in my parents' council house in Derby, not far from the River Derwent. Like most people in the area we were white, proud of it and could trace our family back generations unlike many of the foreign scumbags who lived there now. For this reason, we didn't like niggers, pakis or any of the other foreign scum that the government were letting into the country. We didn't even like the Irish, many of whom had been moving into the area and taking our jobs and women just like the niggers and pakis had been doing in other parts of the country.

I was six years old when I had my first run in with the ethnics as I called them. I had just begun my first year at Ridgeway Infant School and was waiting in the queue for my dinner when this big podgy Irish kid pushed past me and jumped the queue.

"Hey," I cried, "what are you doing? We're queuing here. You'll have to go to the back of the queue."

The kid just turned and punched me. No warning, no provocation. He just punched me, and I wheeled back and crashed into the tray stand.

I was gobsmacked and for a moment just sat there in a bit of a daze. Then I saw blood trickling down my shirt and I went apeshit. I leapt up and began punching him in the head, body and face. I just kept punching and punching and when he hit the ground, I started jumping up and down on his head before kicking him around like a football and smashing a dinner tray over him.

The kid was screaming and there was blood pouring down his face, but I wasn't finished with him yet. This little bastard had struck me for no reason and now he was going to pay for it, so I grabbed a knife and was about to cut him up when I was seized by one of the teachers who snatched the knife out my hand before dragging me yelling and screaming all the way to the headmaster's office.

For that I was sent home and suspended from school for a week, not that my mum and dad cared. The moment they heard that I had kicked the fuck out of an Irish kid, they were overcome with joy. Both were National Front supporters, and both were active within the party, and both were proud that I had beaten up an ethnic.

Indeed, my parents were not only NF supporters but they were quite active within the party. My Father Eddie Hatchet was the local NF Organiser and used to work in the local car factory but lost his job when he was found guilty of glassing a nigger in a pub four years earlier and sent to prison. He was NF through and through and spent his days when he was not signing on the dole, organising NF meetings in Derby, and attending NF demonstrations up and down the country.

My mother, Barbara Hatchet – or Bouncing Barbara as she was known amongst some sections of the local population, due to her dabble in prostitution in her late teens – was also a regular amongst NF demonstrations,. Indeed, it was said that she was even more of a racist than my dad and could often be found at the front of a NF demonstration shouting "niggers out or there's no black in the Union

Jack". Something which remains as true today as it did then, despite the overwhelming influx of ethnics invading our space.

After that altercation with the Irish kid, I quickly got a reputation as a kid you did not mess with and anyone who did always ended up seeing stars with blood pouring out their noses. It was the same at Gayton Juniors and Murray Park Secondary School. Indeed, right on my first day at Murray Park I got myself into a fracas with a youth and he didn't even go to the school.

I was crossing the road after the traffic lights had turned red when this dipstick came flying around the corner and narrowly avoided mowing me down and hordes of other kids. Even then he didn't apologise. Just leaned out his window and yelled, "you stupid bastards" before putting his foot down on the pedal and speeding off.

Then at home time I came across him again. To get to my house from the school, you had to pass through some woodlands and under a large railway bridge and as I approached it, I saw him in the front of his red car parked close by, which surprised me because cars weren't allowed on the footpath as a number of public signs made clear. Still, this dork clearly didn't think the rules applied to him and was one of those people who didn't give a toss about anybody but himself. A bit like me really.

The dork was smoking a spliff and laid back in his chair without a care in the world and did not see me climb up to the bridge and position myself with a brick in my hand directly above him. This prat had come close to running me down this morning and I was determined he was going to pay. So I looked round to make sure the coast was clear before lobbing the brick through his car window and watching gleefully as it smashed into him full on in his face.

I fully expected this prat to jump out of his car yelling "what the fuck" so I ducked behind the bridge wall waiting for him to do so, but there was nothing. Not a sound. I waited and waited but nothing. In fact, the place was that silent, I could swear the birds had stopped singing in the trees. Eventually I felt sufficiently brave to rise from my hiding place and descend the steps and look inside the car and when I did I got a hell of a shock. The dork was dead. His body was laid flat out on the seat and there was blood everywhere. The front seat was also burning, and I realised that when the brick had smashed into his face, the dipstick had dropped his spliff, setting fire to his car. I quickly made a hasty departure.

I like to think that his death played on my mind, but the truth is it didn't. That prick had nearly run me over and may well have killed me, without any thought for my wellbeing so why should I worry about his? Still, I was on edge all that night. I kept thinking the police would knock on the door and take me away. They didn't, and the next day I virtually ran to school but when I got to the pass, I was stopped in my tracks. The police were everywhere. Hordes of them were just poking in and out of the bushes, hoping the killer had left something that would leave a clue as to his identity. I knew I hadn't and so wasn't worried about that but what did worry me was when I saw police officers on the bridge. I thought, shit, did I leave a footprint when I was up there tossing the brick down. I mean, I could explain my footprints being on the path because I took that route to and from school every day. But up there was another matter, and I knew all about footprints because of some crime programme I had recently watched on tv.

Then a police officer told me and the rest of the kids who were stood there gawping to move on and take a different route to school, which we did. Once there everybody was talking about the murder, including a number of kids I hung around with. One of them was Ian Simpson or Simsy as we called him. He was a tall, lanky lad, a bit slow on the uptake with a tendency to rabble on a bit.

"Hey, Harry," he cried, when he saw me hurrying towards him across the playground. "Some lad's been murdered down on the footpath. A drug dealer by the name of Neil Dogson. Ever heard of him?"

I shook my head, clearly fascinated to discover the name of the dork I had killed. "Who murdered him, do the police know?"

"Dunno, mate, but the word is it was a drug deal gone wrong. Anyway, that's the story going around the school."

Was it? How encouraging. I only hoped the police believed it, but it soon became clear that they were leaving all options open because at assembly time we were addressed by the police officer in charge of the investigation. A scrawny looking man who introduced himself as Chief Inspector Dereck Bell. Not to put too fine a point on it, he said his officers would be interviewing all the kids during the day, to see if they had seen or heard anything that may be relevant to the case, but it was nothing to worry about, it was just routine enquiries. Then he stunned everybody by asking if anybody had thrown a brick into the car as a prank and finished off by saying that if they had, they must say now or come to the headmaster's office after assembly where the matter could be dealt with without any further ado.

There were gasps all round when he said that, because none of the other kids seemed to have considered the possibility that one of their fellow pupils might be responsible for the murder, despite it taking place on a wooded path at the back of the school. In fact, looking around the assembly hall, some of the teachers looked shocked by the suggestion as well.

So throughout that day, all the kids were interviewed at some stage and I learned later they put the same questions to them as they did to me.

"Did you see the victim sitting in his car? Was he with anybody? Did you see him talking to anybody out of the car? Who did you see in the woods? Was that person acting strangely? Did you climb up to the bridge? Did you see anybody on the bridge? Has anybody's behaviour today struck you as odd? Have you heard anybody boasting of the murder or talking about it in a way which made you think they know more than they should?"

I said I hadn't seen anything other than the victim sat in his car smoking what looked like a spliff. I hadn't spoken to him and hadn't seen him talking to anybody, but I had only glimpsed him briefly and it was possible there was somebody else in his car, but I didn't see anyone.

While all this was going on, the clock on the wall was ticking away and I was concerned that as I had been walking home alone, the police would treat me as a bigger suspect than those who had been walking home in a group and could testify for each other's actions, but strangely enough they didn't and hey presto, that was it and the interview was over.

I was surprised but I later found out that the police didn't think any of the kids were responsible, but they had to interview us all in case they were wrong. They believed he really was killed in a drug deal gone wrong. Sounds strange but that's how it was and who was I to argue. Besides, after I gave my statement, another thought occurred to me. What if I left my fingerprints on the car or on the brick? If so, I would have some pretty difficult questions to face. Luckily for me, the dork had dropped his spliff when the brick smashed into his face (as I said earlier), causing the vehicle to set alight and burn him and it to a cinder, destroying any evidence in the process.

NATIONAL FRONT

So, on my first day at Murray Park Secondary School, I committed murder and got away with it. Now that's not something every kid can boast about, is it? Still, I couldn't just sit there and gloat about it, I had to get on with the rest of my life and that was not violent free, I assure you. In fact, for the next few weeks I felt like I was living at the O.K. Corral. It's an odd thing, but boys love to fight, well, many of us do anyway, and when we start a new school all of us want to prove we are the hardest in the year. At my school they weren't, I was, as any kid who fancied their chances soon found out and there is always one or two mugs who fancy their chances, isn't there?

First up was a lad called Ian Riley or fatty Riley as I called him given the fat bastard was over fifteen stone and wobbled wherever he went. This fat bastard had been cock of his junior school and had recently beaten the cock of another junior school, Tommy Rawlins, the previous week. He was no match for me, not that he knew it. Well, not then anyway. He found me out one dinner time when I was having a fag with me mates behind the bike shed and I immediately accepted.

"Right then," he said, poking a podgy finger at me and casting a smirk at the crew he brought with him. "I'll see you after school on the embankment and don't be late or I'll come looking for ya."

In those days most fights took place on the embankment. The reason for it is that it was beyond the school gates so the teachers didn't get involved as they did for example when fights broke out in the classroom or on the playground and you could go at it hammer or tongues without anyone breaking it up. For that reason, I could well understand why fights were held there. What I couldn't fathom was why this fat bastard thought I was going to wait until then to knock his head off given we were behind the bike sheds and there wasn't a teacher in sight.

So I leapt forward and headbutted him, causing him to wheel backwards and crash into the wall with blood spouting outta his nose, too shocked to do anything but slide to the ground and lie there with his head tilted to one side as though out for the count. In fact, I'm sure he was but I wasn't finished with him yet. This bastard had not only challenged me but had threatened me with consequences if I didn't show, and nobody threatens me. So I laid into him with my fists and boots, kicking him so hard in the head, body and face, that all of his mates were looking on alarmed and one or two were muttering under their breaths but I told them to shut it or I would do them too before turning back to Fatty and beating him to pulp.

Second up, Kevan Watts. This prat had also been cock of his junior school and was in fact an area school boy boxing champion after winning the Derbyshire juniors boxing championships a couple of weeks back and when we met on the embankment a couple of days after I beat fatty Riley to a pulp, it showed. The kid hit me with a couple of well-timed punches which I must admit did knock me backwards and send me tumbling backwards onto my arse, but that was the difference between him and me. He was a boxer whereas I was a street fighter. He played by the Marquis of Queensbury's rules whereas I didn't play by any rules and never wanted to. He was expecting a fight where two kids would exchange a series of punches until only one was standing, while with me anything goes. Head, fist, elbow, foot, you name it, I would use it if it helped me win a fight. I would even smash an iron bar down on your head, or some other object, but whatever I did to win, trust me, I would do it as Watts was just about to discover.

Jumping up, I surged forward and booted him so hard in the kneecap he let out an almighty wail and hit the deck clutching his knee in agony. I was wearing Doctor Marten boots with steel toe caps, so it wasn't surprising he was on the deck rolling about in agony, but I wasn't about to let up. I kicked him in the head, body and face and then pulled him up by the neck and threw in a couple of punches for good measure. I was like a wild animal just hitting and hitting, and nobody could stop me, not the horde of older kids looking on and staring at me and each over in disbelief as the blood continued to gush out of Watts' nose, not Simsy and the rest of the crew, not even the masses of girls wearing short skirts and white shirts standing next to some of the older lads and muttering to themselves. Eventually I let go of Watts' neck and booted him one more time in the face before pushing everybody out the way and leaving Watts splat out on the ground.

My third and final opponent was Trevor Mullholland. He wasn't so much hard as big. He was a towering six foot two, which, given we were only eleven years old at the time, was huge. Still, this was another fight which did not take place on the embankment as it was supposed to. He challenged me to a fight one dinner time in the boys' toilets and then pulled something outta his pocket and said, "Oh yes, I'll be using this."

I said, "What the fuck's that?"

He said, "It's a knuckle duster, dickhead. What the fuck do you think it is?"

I said, "A knuckle duster. Let me see," before snatching it from him and smashing it full on in his face. His eyes nearly popped out his head and he hit the deck looking somewhat bog-eyed, but I just punched and punched until eventually he was flat out on the floor and that was it. I was cock of year seven and everybody knew it.

For the next three years at school, I was in and out of trouble on a fairly regular basis, partly because history, maths and all the other crap they taught us, bored me to bits, and partly because it was more fun messing about and winding the teachers up than sitting there and listening to them drone on and on. All of them were a target and all of them hated me, but none more than Cohen who taught maths over in the E block. I used to wind him up more than anyone else, not only because he was an annoying little weasel who used to rap your knuckles with a ruler when you misbehaved but also because he was Jewish and therefore just another one of those ethnic scumbags plaguing our country by their presence. I used to place swastikas on his car and cut his car tyres with a knife while Simsy and the rest of crew stood nearby making sure I wasn't caught. Then, I found out that his parents had died at Auschwitz, and his brother, sister, aunty and grandparents at Treblinka so I left a picture of dead Jews on his car window after they had been gassed and wrote underneath, *recognise your grandparents and other family members do you?*.

It was absolutely hilarious but not as hilarious as when the man saw it and went ape shit. He thought a lad called Keven Garrett had done it because the stupid bastard just happened to be lurking nearby and lashed out at the eejit, breaking his nose and putting the bozo in hospital, which in turn led to him being arrested for assault, sacked from his job and eventually barred from entering the teaching profession again. As I said, hilarious.

During weekends I was just as unruly. My family lived on the notoriously violent Mackworth estate which was a poor rundown council area about a mile or so from the school and high in social depravation, poverty and crime. You name it, every kind of skulduggery you can think of went on down there from drug dealing, robbery and prostitution to even the occasional murder. I used to spend my weekends getting pissed with Simsy and the rest of my crew at the back of the estate on booze which we either nicked from the local off licence or which the owner gave us at a discount price to stop us nicking it in the first place. Sometimes if it was raining we would pop down to the local youth club where I would spend my time drinking, smoking, sniffing glue and playing snooker and other times I would be back home in my room shagging every girl I took a fancy to, and why not, may I ask. I mean, let's face it, ladies, don't I sound like a real charmer to you? Don't I sound like the sort of boy you would love to have taken home to your parents and said to them, "Look, Mum and Dad. This is Harry Hatchet. Harry's my boyfriend. What a lovely boy he is, aren't I lucky to have him?" Well, come on, don't I?

Because my dad was the NF organiser, it was his job to hire coaches to take him and other NF members in the area to demonstrations up and down the county and when that happened and they had to travel overnight in order to get to the demo on time, I would go and stay at my grandparents' house on the other side of town and that was quite a treat, I can tell you. My grandmother, Maria Hatchet, was an excellent cook and she made the most wonderful steak and kidney puddings, apple tarts and other scrumptious delights and I ate like a king when I was there. But it was the stories that my grandfather told me after we had eaten, and he was sat in his favourite armchair next to the sizzling fire reminiscing about old times that I enjoyed the most.

You may not believe this but my grandfather, Charlie Hatchet, was a leading member of the British Union of Fascists (BUF) and was so dedicated to the movement that Oswald Mosley himself, the party's infamous leader, chose him to be his official bodyguard and with good reason. My grandfather wasn't just a dedicated party member but the best streetfighter there was. In his youth he had earned his living as a bare fist fighter and taken on some of the hardest men in the country and won. On one occasion he had knocked out the bare fist champion in Norfolk with just one punch, and then a month later, beat the bare fist champion of Liverpool in less than five minutes, despite the latter being considered the hardest man in the country at the time. He was even present at the Battle of the Cable Street in October 1936 when hordes of anarchists, communists, Jews, socialists and other unwashed scum tried to prevent Mosley and the rest of the BUF marching few Cable Street and other parts of East London wearing their black shirts and Nazi emblems but the BUF stood their ground and smashed them out of the way before continuing to march through the area with Mosley and my Grandfather at their head.

But it was when my grandfather travelled with Mosley and meet my hero, Adolf Hitler, in the early 1930s that really enthralled me. Can you believe it? My grandfather actually met Adolf Hitler, a man I worshipped as a god. A man whose portrait hung on my bedroom wall next to the huge swastika flag I cherished beside it.

I used to sit there tugging at his sleeve and say to my granddad, "What was it like? What was it like when you met my hero?" and he would swell his chest up with pride and say with a tear in his eye, "Harry, it was the proudest moment in my life as he was the greatest man that ever lived."

In fact, it was my grandfather who first persuaded my dad to take me on my first NF march. Up until then Dad had been reluctant because I was only a kid and such events often turned into pitch battles between the NF and red scum who turned out to oppose them and he didn't want me getting hurt. Personally, I thought my dad was simply being soft but I found out later that if he had taken me on a march and I had ended up getting hurt and put in hospital, he would have had the police, social services and every other do-gooder down on him like a ton of bricks alleging child neglect and I may well have been taken away and put in a foster home, so it wasn't a case of him being soft, but simply protective.

Still, my grandfather talked him round. He pointed out that I had recently turned sixteen and as such was now nearing the age where I would be too old to be put in a foster home and not only that, but I was six feet three with the muscles and strength to go with it. So any allegation of child neglect simply would simply be laughed out of court.

I was lucky, very lucky. It wasn't until two months later that the NF held another march and when they did it was at Lewisham on 13 August 1977 and everybody or anybody who was involved with the NF at the time will tell you the significance of that date for the events that day would go down in NF folklore as the Battle of Lewisham and yours truly was right in the thick of it.

It began quietly enough. A coach took me and all the other local NF members to Lewisham, a borough in South London where we disembarked and made our way to Achilles Street where NF supporters from all around the country were assembling. There were hordes of NF supporters there, mostly skinheads in their late teens, wearing jeans, white shirts and red braces, but quite a few older guys, including one guy wearing a suit and tie who was addressing the crowd and clearly running the show.

I said to Simsy, "Who the fuck is that?" but he didn't know, then one of the skinheads who was standing in front of me wearing a white shirt with Millwall NF written on it turned around and said, "That's John Tyndall, dickhead, the Chairman of the National Front. Who the fuck do you think it is?"

He turned back to his mates with a sneer, so I tapped him on his shoulder and when he turned back, butted him so hard in the face he just hit the deck quicker than you could say jack shit. As quick as a flash the space around me opened up and his mates turned to me with clenched fists and angry growls on their faces.

"Oh aye," I said, curling my lips back in a sardonic grin, "fancy your chances, do you? Well, come on then."

I went to lunge at them, but some old geezer blocked my path. "Don't, son," he said, glancing at me with a look of alarm on his face. "They're the NF Leader Guard, you don't want to mess with them."

"The NF Leader guard," I said, puzzled. "Who the fuck are they?"

"They're Mr Tyndall's personal bodyguards and the hardest of the hardest, trust me, you don't want to mess with them."

I burst out laughing. "Hardest of the hard. They look like a bunch of wankers to me," I cried, before pushing him out the way and turning back to them. But again, my path was blocked. This time by John Tyndall himself.

"Who the devil are you and what the devil do you think you are playing at?" he yelled.

I stared at him. The man looked like a toff. Dressed like a toff and spoke like a toff and I wasn't sure whether to bow or punch him. Either way I didn't get the chance. The was a large commotion behind me and a couple of police officers came barging through. At first I thought they were coming to arrest me for headbutting that gobby git who was being helped to his feet by his mates but it was the NF leader they were after.

"Right, Mr Tyndall, you can begin your march now," one said, "but be warned, there are thousands of anti-fascists protestors in town and they are baying for blood."

"Oh good," I cried, clenching my fist and curling my lips back into a grin. "So now we can stop pissing about and go and put the bastards in hospital, or even better, chop off their heads and put them on lamp posts like they did in medieval times."

Both Tyndall and the police officers looked at me as though I wasn't quite right in the head but before anybody could say anything, there was a shifting of feet behind me and that was it, we were off.

I wasn't surprised that the red scum had turned out in large numbers to oppose us. For weeks they had been trying to get the march banned on the grounds that it would lead to public disorder as many of the locals did not want the NF marching in the area and spreading their message of hate. Some, like the Mayor of Lewisham, the Bishop of Southwark and the local Liberal party, had even written to the

Commissioner of the Metropolitan Police, David McNee, asking him to apply to the Home Secretary for a ban to be imposed but he refused to do so on the grounds that if a ban were imposed it would lead to "increasing pressure" to ban similar events and would be "abdicating his responsibility in the face of groups who threaten to achieve their ends by violent means." By that he meant he would be caving into all those socialist wankers who had threatened to stop the march by fair means or foul if it did go ahead. Something the anti-fascists proved intent on doing anyway.

No sooner had we walked about a hundred yards than the reds came swarming down at us from all directions. It was like a scene from *Zulu Dawn* with hordes of unwashed scum descending on us like a pack of wild lotus. I had my first glance of the Anti Nazi League, with their yellow lollipops and ANL written on them and I said to Simsy, "Who the fuck do they think they are trying to scare? They look like lollipop men and women to me."

There was laughter all round and then the Social Workers Party (SWP) – or Social Wankers Party as they are known – put in an appearance. I knew they would. They were a pathetic bunch of left wing loonies who took it upon themselves to harass the NF whenever they stood in elections or held a march and most of them could not punch their way out of a paperback bag let alone take part in a decent street fight. In fact, most were students, hippies, faggots or sometimes all three, and as they got closer carrying their SWP placards, I was looking forward to smashing one down over their scrawny heads.

In fact, I was dying to but there were tons of police officers between us and them and the police were keeping us caged in like sardines in a can. The number of police officers on duty that day was not sufficient to keep things from spiraling out of control and within minutes bricks, bottles, and a variety of other objects were reigning down on us like meteorites out of the sky. Some of them hit their targets and I saw one or two NF members dropping down clutching their heads with blood pouring down their faces, but I wasn't fazed. Instead, I grabbed a dustbin lid to use as a shield and then turned to the NF and yelled, "What the fuck are you stood there for? Attack!" before smashing the lid down into the face of a red who had broken through police lines and was lunging at us with a bottle in hand.

He quickly saw stars as did a couple of other reds behind him who I kicked, punched, nutted, or booted out the way. For a while it was touch and go as both sides fought pitched battles in the street as neither side seemed to get the better of the other. We had the best fighters, but they had the sheer numbers and for every red we downed, two appeared in their place. I continued to punch, kick, nut and down every red in my way but our numbers were going down as NF members started dropping like flies and eventually we started to get overwhelmed and I was eventually overpowered by the mob and thrown head first few a shop window as indeed were other NF members they got their hands on.

"Fascist scum," they shouted as the glass shattered around us.

"Nazi scum of our streets," yelled another rabble behind them.

Some NFs were begging for mercy and pleading with the crowd not to hurt them, even those who had been thrown few a window but not me. Unfortunately, for them they had thrown me few the window of a shop that sold mock armaments and my hands fell on a pair of hatchets made outta rubber. I say rubber, but it was pretty hard stuff and one whack from that and you would be seeing stars for a week. Still, I couldn't care less what they were made of. They were weapons and I intended to use them so I grabbed them and jumped back out the window and yelled, "Who's first?"

  The anti-fascists froze. Took one look at my bloody attire and the fact I was holding what appeared to be a pair of hatchets and fled for their lives. Some, however, couldn't get away quickly enough because there were too many people in front of them and ended up tripping over each over, and I laid into them with everything I had. I whacked men and women, young and old, big or small, I didn't care. If they were there they got it. Eventually, though, the police regained control and we were marched back to our coaches and sent on our way, well, at least those who could walk were. Those who couldn't were either taken away in ambulances or treated on the spot.

  I was absolutely buzzing when I got home but that wasn't the end of the matter. The next day the papers were full of information on the previous day's event, labelling it the Battle of Lewisham' and calling it an absolute disgrace that such unruly behavior could break out on the streets of London. They even had pictures of both the NFs and the anti-fascists attacking each other with bricks, sticks and knives and went on to suggest that the events had been hijacked by lunatics on both sides of the political spectrum. How else could one explain the utter carnage that we witnessed on the streets of Lewisham yesterday, one newspaper asked.

I was over the moon when I read it because I considered it an utter privilege to have been there and given the reds a lesson they would never forget, but then I got the shock of my life. When the police had marched us back to our coaches an elderly gent with a camera and reporter written all over him had come up to me and said, "You put up a good fight there, son. What's your name?"

"Harry Hatchet," I replied, my chest swelling up with pride.

What I didn't realise at the time was that he had been taking pictures of me earlier on and to my utter astonishment, there I was on the front cover of some of the country's most read newspapers with blood splattered all over me, holding a pair of hatchets and wading into a group of anti-fascist protestors.

Hatchet Harry confronts the mob was the headline in one newspaper.

Hatchet Harry takes on baying mob said another.

Hatchet Harry in action, wrote yet another.

I said to my dad, "What the fuck are they calling me Hatchet Harry for, my name is Harry Hatchet" and he just said, "That's the media for you. They like a good soundbite and what with your name being Harry Hatchet and your holding a pair of hatchets, it's just a clever use of your name to sell papers."

Clever or not, it was certainly a shock but I wasn't complaining and in fact I was made up to know that people up and down the country were talking about me and glancing at pictures of me confronting the red scum. Still, it wouldn't be the last time my exploits made national headlines. Soon I would be making them again, this time for attacking, chopping up and burying the body parts of football hooligans who pissed me off, including those who belonged to those cockney wankers otherwise known as West Ham Inter City Firm.

HOOLIGAN

It was by chance I became a football hooligan. My dad had organised an NF demonstration in Birmingham to protest at the pakis taking over the place and I couldn't wait to go along and join in. I thought, if it's anything like Lewisham it would be too good to miss.

We went on a coach and the seats were filled with some faces I did know, and others I did not. When we got to our destination the place was swarming with police officers and the usual array of unwashed scum from the Anti Nazi League (ANL), Social Workers Party (SWP), and God knows what waving their banners and shouting, "Nazi Scum of our Streets."

I immediately sprang forward to attack them, as did the rest of my NF mates, but the police beat us back with truncheons and forced us to confront them from a distance, which was very annoying for us but lucky for them, because if it had come down to a fist fight it would not have taken us long to put them all in hospital. They were a rabble, they really were, weaklings who couldn't punch their way out of a paper bag but who felt safe to confront you because there were hordes of police officers stood between them and you.

I yelled at one particular gobby git, a hippy who looked as though he hadn't had a bath for a week, "You're very brave with the police stood in front of you, aren't you? Tell you what. Why don't you and I go somewhere and have a one to one, now. Come on, how about it?"

Well, he didn't want to know of course, despite giving me the V sign and big I am. So I shook my head, pulled out my Union Jack and stood yelling, "There's no black in the Union Jack."

On the way home, things were different. We had just pulled into a motorway service station when two vans pulled up beside us and a bunch of hard-looking characters jumped out and began lobbing bricks through the windows. I was so taken aback I dropped the spliff I was smoking and crouched down, trying to shield myself from the bricks and shattering glass.

"What the hell's going on?" I heard somebody shout.

"It's the reds," shouted another. "They're pelting us with bricks."

"Then let's get them," I yelled, trampling over bodies and yanking open the door.

God knows how I managed to avoid the bricks that were still hurling through the window but when I jumped off the coach, these red scumbags got the fright of their lives.

"Right," I yelled, headbutting one unwashed goon out the way and laying another out with one punch. "Fancy your chances, do you? Well, let's get to it."

I streamed into them and began knocking out one red goon after another. Some of these guys were big boys and one grabbed me from behind and lifted me into the air before throwing me into the side of the van. I quickly got up and punched him so hard he wobbled back and fell on his feet before the sound of police sirens waded through the air and everybody, including me, jumped back on the coach and made a quick getaway.

Once clear of the service station, the coach was full of people torn between those cursing the far left scum who had attacked us and those congratulating me on putting up a heroic defence. One lad, a vicious-looking skinhead with a scar on his face, was more complimentary than any of the others.

"That was good stuff, mate," he said, patting me on the shoulder and fixing me with a firm smile. "Who are ya?"

"That's Eddy Hatchet's son," a voice cried from behind. "Harry."

"What, Hatchet Harry," the skinhead said, staring at me with a look of awe. "Christ, I've heard of you. You're the guy who attacked the red scum in Lewisham with a couple of hatchets, aren't you?"

I nodded. "And who are you?" I said, taking in the familiar jeans, white shirt, red braces and Doctor Marten boots, which NF members tended to wear a lot in those days, largely because many skinheads were passionate followers of mod culture and mod culture was quite the rage at the time, and also because many of them had far right sympathies and it was not uncommon to see them on NF marches wearing such attire.

"I'm Biffo," he said, his chest swelling with pride. "I'm the leader of the Derby Fairy Cakes."

I burst out laughing. "The who?"

"The Derby Fairy Cakes," he repeated. "It's the name of Derby County's hooligan firm."

"Hooligan firm," I said. "What fucking hooligan firm?"

So he explained. It turned out the Derby Fairy Cakes were a bunch of violent thugs who followed Derby County up and down the country, not to watch them play but to fight other hooligan firms whenever their teams met. It seemed every club in the Vauxhall League had them, which, back in the seventies, was equivalent to the Premier League, and every hooligan firm was eager to prove that their firm was the hardest and toughest around. As such, battles would often break out between rival firms and when they did they would often resemble a medieval battle with both sets of firms streaming into each other with knives, bricks, bottles, and what other weapons they could get their hands on. It was clearly up my street, and I knew I was going to get involved right then and there but one thing puzzled me, and I turned to this Biffo with a frown on my face.

"Why the fuck do you call yourselves the Derby Fairy Cakes?" I said with a slight frown. "Sounds like a bunch of queers to me. You're not a bunch of queers, are you? Because I hate fucking queers. They make me sick. In fact, if it was up to me I'd gas the fucking lot of them like Hitler did with the Jews."

There was a roar of laughter when I said that, and I hadn't realised the whole coach had gone quiet and was hanging on to my every word. Biffo too was laughing but his was a kind of nervous laugh and he was looking at me as though he thought I had escaped from Rampton or some other mental institution. Anyway, he said they weren't a bunch of queers and after reassuring me on that point, I asked him to tell me more about the Derby Fairy Cakes and football hooliganism in general, which he did.

It turned out that football hooliganism had a long history in England and went back to the 1880s when individuals referred to as roughs used to cause trouble at football matches by attacking opponents with boots, fists, or whatever weapons they could get their hands on. Unlike today, however, most fights took place between hooligans from local teams as this was an era where most people did not have the time or money to travel up and down the country engaging in fist fights with thugs from different parts of the realm. Indeed, it was for this reason that many of these fights broke out on Derby days, as was the case, for example, in 1889 when violence broke out between rival gangs from Liverpool and Everton FC, leading to one man, Henry Tobin, getting stabbed to death and an Everton hooligan by the name of Joseph Towns being charged, tried and convicted of murder, before being hung at the gallows despite pleas of mercy to the Home Secretary and Queen Victoria, which went unheeded.

By the 1960s, however, things were starting to change. Thanks to a better transport system and working conditions, hooligans had both the time and money to travel around the country and even abroad to engage in pitch battles with rival hooligans. In 1962, for example, an assortment of English hooligans ran amok when England played France at the Stade Vélodrome, leading to Charles De Gaulle dubbing hooliganism 'the Englishman's disease.'

But it was in the early 1970s when firms whose names have since become synonymous with hooliganism stared to emerge, such as Aston Villa's C-Crew, Stoke City's Naughty Forty and Portsmouth 6.57 Crew.

I said to Biffo, "The 6.57 crew, what's all that about? Why do Portsmouth call themselves the 6.57 crew?"

And he said, "It's British rail, Harry. There's a train that leaves Portsmouth every day for London Euston at 6.57 sharp, and as the Portsmouth lads use it to get to away games, they decided to call themselves the 6.57 crew. Simple, isn't it."

It certainly was but that still did not explain why Derby's hooligans called themselves the Derby Fairy Cakes. I mean, the whole thing was a farce, wasn't it? Who the hell is going to take a bunch of hooligans seriously if they call themselves the Fairy Cakes? Other firms would probably burst out laughing at the mere mention of your name. I know I would if I heard the Derby Fairy Cakes were in town and looking to have a ruck with my crew. For Biffo, however, the name made perfect sense.

"The local connection," he said, his voice bursting with pride. "We call ourselves the Fairy Cakes because we used to have a big factory in Derby that made fairy cakes and we thought it would be a great idea to call ourselves after the factory and highlight our connection to the area. Besides," he said, his face breaking out into a grin, "we did it for a laugh. We did it so other firms would not take us seriously until we put them in hospital and then we could tell everyone, look, the

Chelsea Headhunters have been done over by the Derby Fairy Cakes, or any other firm silly enough to take us on."

This time it was my turn to wonder if it was him who had escaped from some lunatic asylum, but he wasn't finished yet. Hooligans like nothing more than talking about their exploits, me included, which is why I have written this book, and throughout the journey he told me how Derby's hooligan firm had been striking fear into rival firms since they were formed in 1970.

One of their first successes he told me, took place on 8 August 1970, when hordes of Manchester United's fans went on the rampage in Derby town centre after Derby County beat Manchester United 4—1 in the Watney Cup.

"It was brilliant, Harry," he said, his chest swilling up with pride. "It really was. The Red Army, that's Man United's hooligan firm, kicked off as soon as the ref blown the whistle and began throwing missiles onto the pitch and at us. Then when we chased them out the ground, they started squirting ammonia at us which they had brought with them in bottles before legging it through the town centre and going on the rampage. They kicked in shop window after shop window before we caught up with them and give these Man United skinheads a lesson they would never forget."

"Skinheads," I said, puzzled. "Man United's hooligan firm comprise of skinheads, yet they call themselves the Red Army. How can that be? Reds are hippies, niggers, students and other left wing scum. How can skinheads be involved with the reds? I thought skinheads are NF like you and me."

Again there was a roar of laughter and Biffo hastened to explain.

"No, Harry, you don't understand. Man United's firm are called the Red Army because their team plays in red. But still, you're right about them being made up of left wing scumbags. In fact, many of them are members of the Social Workers Party, including the skinheads."

"But why?" I said, still confused. "Why would skinheads want to be members of the Social Workers Party?"

"Dunno, mate," said Biffo. "It's a mystery to me too. But they do."

I would like to have asked him more but right then we arrived back home and Biffo had to dash off because he had a date with some girl he had recently met in a chip shop but before he went, he told me Derby County were playing Coventry on Saturday away and said if I wanted to join him and the rest of the Derby Fairy Cakes in kicking hell out of their firm, I was to meet him at ten o'clock at the train station.

Come the day, I turned up on time which was a miracle because by now I was signing on the dole and never got out of bed until midday. Still, what Biffo told me about football hooliganism excited me so much I just had to be there and as soon as I arrived, I was in for a disappointment. Biffo was nowhere to be seen. Nor anybody who looked as though they might be up for a bit of football violence. The only people who were there were men in smart suits and other members of the public going about their lawful business.

I turned to Simsy with a frown on my face and said, "If that bastard Biffo has got me out my pit for no reason, I'll have him."

Then a kid came flying round the corner on a bike, clocked us, and came to a screeching halt. For a few seconds he just stared as us although he was checking us out. Then he turned on his bike, shot across the road to the pub, and plonked his bike down, before scurrying off inside.

For a few minutes nothing happened, and I was just debating with myself whether I should nick his bike and sell it on to one of the kids on my estate when the door of the pub was yanked back and out came a group of lads clutching bottles and wearing Derby County shirts.

"Who the fuck are you?" one yelled. "Want a go, do ya?"

"It's Coventry's firm," cried another. "They've come here hoping to catch us by surprise."

I said to Simsy. "Coventry firm? What the fuck are they talking about? Where are the Coventry firm?"

"They think we are," said Simsy, eyeing up the baying mob nervously, "and that we were planning on attacking them while they were drinking in the pub. At least that's what that kid must have told them."

I glanced at the kid who was just stood there with a sort of gloating look in his eye and looking very pleased with himself. I rushed forward and booted him so hard up the backside that he virtually flew up in the air and crashed down onto some bins looking somewhat bog-eyed as he did. Then I turned to the Derby crew who were looking shell shocked I had attacked a twelve-year-old boy with such violence that they were unsure what to do next.

Then this overweight buffoon stepped forward with a bottle in his hand and yelled, "That's my son you just assaulted, you bastard."

"Shut it," I cried, punching him so hard he was soon joining his son on the deck.

Then I started laying into the rest of them as did Simsy and the rest of my crew and very soon the Fairy Cakes were either hitting the deck, fleeing back into the pub or legging it down the street. I was just about to smash a bottle over somebody's head when a car came to a screeching halt and out jumped Biffo, red faced and yelling, "No, Harry, don't. He's one of us."

I pulled back and as I did, I heard somebody say, "Harry. You mean this is Hatchet Harry? Christ, I didn't realise it was him."

The man stared at me with a look of awe on his face and when he spoke, you could hear the fear in his voice.

"Sorry, Harry, we didn't know it was you, we thought you lot were the Coventry firm come to do us over."

"What!" said Biffo incredulously. "When we're playing Coventry away. For God's sake, you morons, surely it's obvious their firm will try to ambush us on their home turf not here."

Well, whether or not they would or wouldn't wasn't the subject of further discussion as a train pulled in to the station across the road and we all piled on it, minus the guys who had legged down the street of course, and the father and son who were still looking a bit bogeyed and being helped into the car which had brought Biffo.

It was possible that they were on their way to the police station to complain I had assaulted them, but I somewhat doubted it. The father had attacked me with a bottle in his hand. How could he explain that to the police without dropping himself in it and as for his son, well, I doubt he would say anything, unless the little bastard wanted to find himself being dragged down a dark alley and having his legs broken and tongue cut out for grassing me up to the police, that is.

COVENTRY

The trip to Coventry took less than fifty minutes and it wasn't long before we pulled into the train station and disembarked along with other Derby fans who had made the trip with us. I had never been to this city before, but I knew one or two things about it. I knew that the Luftwaffe had bombed it during the Blitz, and that Lady Godiva had driven naked through the town, but that was about it. Still, the first thing that struck me as odd was the mass of police officers loitering about outside the station.

I said to Biffo, "What the fuck's going on? Is Ronny Kray in town or what?"

But he just laughed and said, "No, Harry, this is match day and the police are always out in large numbers to keep order and ensure fighting does not break out between rival fans."

We walked out the station and turned right down the road. Biffo clearly knew the way to the ground because he said it wasn't far to Highfield Road where Coventry played their home games but even if he didn't, it wouldn't have been too hard to find our way there. All we needed to do was to follow the endless parade of people wearing Derby scarves, who were being escorted to the ground by the police.

I said to Biffo, "Where the hell are the Coventry's firm, are they waiting for us at the ground or what?"

He shook his head. "Doubt it, Harry," he said, glancing briefly at his watch. "The game doesn't start till three. They'll be in their local boozer getting sloshed at the moment."

I said, "Let's go there."

"We are, Harry," he replied with a slight snigger, "it's just opposite the ground."

For the next ten minutes we continued on down the road but then as the stadium came into sight, I noticed some of the Coventry fans on the opposite side of the road were looking at us and mumbling amongst themselves.

I said to Biffo, "What's the fuck's wrong with them? Do they want it or what?"

Biffo smiled. "It's because we're Derby, Harry. Some of their fans like to give it the big I am when they're surrounded by police officers, just like the reds do at NF marches."

We continued on and arrived outside Highfield Road about five minutes later. The place was absolutely heaving with Coventry fans and many of them were giving us the evil eye and calling us scum.

I said to a particularly gobby git, "Want a go, do you? Well, come on then." But he just backtracked and disappeared into the crowd.

Then Biffo pointed out the pub which the Coventry firm hang out in, so I said, "Let's go in and surprise them," but it was too late. Apparently, they had some spotters outside keeping an eye out for us and the minute they clocked us they rushed inside and barracked the door.

I immediately leapt forward and began pounding on it furiously. "Let us in you cowards," I cried, "we've come to have a one to one with your firm."

No reply.

"Let us in," I yelled, continuing to bang furiously on the door.

Still no reply.

Then a window above me opened and I saw a tough-looking character in his thirties with a rugged jaw stick his neck out. "Who the fuck are you?" he cried.

"We're the Derby Fairy Cakes," I replied.

"The who?" he said, smiling.

"The Derby Fairy Cakes," I replied. "We've come to have it out with your firm."

This time there was a roar of laughter from within the pub and the man smiled even more.

"Sorry," he said, wiping a tear from his eye. "We don't eat fairy cakes until tea time. Come back later."

Again there was the sound of laughter within the pub and I waved an angry fist at him. "Listen you little ponce," I yelled, "stop pissing me about and get down here now."

He refused to do so, so I picked up a brick and was about to lob it through the window, when there was the sound of yelling behind me and a group of police officers came running up.

"You there," one yelled. "What do you think you are doing?"

"Just trying to get a drink," I said, thinking fast on my feet and discarding the brick. "But the door is locked."

"Place is full of Coventry fans," said the guy out the window. "This lot are the Derby Fairy Cakes and will get eaten for dinner if they go inside. We eat fairy cakes for tea," he added with a slight grin.

I would've loved to have wiped that smirk off his grubby face, but the police moved us on and we were frog marched over to the stadium and over to where all the other Derby fans were queuing up to pay the entrance fee. Once inside I had my first glimpse of the ground.

It's a funny thing but up until then I had never set foot in a football ground in my life, despite the fact that back in the seventies, Derby had quite a good team and many of my schoolmates used to get taken to the baseball ground every time Derby played at home. I suppose it was because my dad was not interested in football and was far too busy with his NF activities to take me to home games, as other boys' dads did, and I wasn't interested in football anyway. I much preferred fighting, sniffing glue or chasing girls on the estate.

The first thing that caught my eye as soon as I got in was the vast numbers of people here. I mean, I had seen football matches on television so was fully aware they attracted large numbers but all the same I was astounded by how many people there were. There must have been twenty, thirty, possibly even forty thousand people here, perhaps even more. What's more, the tide of light blue scarves seemed to stretch around the ground and I said to Biffo, "What do we do now? I didn't come here to watch football, I came here to have a fight with Coventry's firm. So, let's get back to that pub and do them."

Hatchet Harry

Biffo just laughed and said, "There will be no point because they will have made their way here by now and standing on the south side behind the goals as they always do."

So I said, "Good, let's get at them."

That, however, was easily said than done. The police escorted us over to where all the over Derby fans were standing, but the problem was to get there the police had to take us round the side of the pitch as the Derby fans were on the other side, which meant running a gantlet of abuse from the Coventry fans as we did.

"Scumbags," the Coventry fans yelled, as Biffo and others began waving their Derby scarves and trying to wind up the crowd. "Scumbags," they yelled again as Biffo and his mates continued to goad them.

Then we passed the south side of the goal and hordes of Coventry fans began going absolutely nuts.

"Fucking scum," cried one person.

"Pricks," cried another.

"It's the Legion," said Biffo. "Coventry's hooligan outfit."

"The Legion," I said, puzzled. "Why do they call themselves the Legion?"

"It's their top boy," replied Biffo, pausing in the act of yelling abuse at the Coventry rabble. "He's a nut on the Roman era so he decided to call his firm the Legion – as in Legion of Roman solders."

I gave him a look and he nodded in agreement. "Yeah, silly isn't it. But that's football hooliganism for you."

I was barely listening. Just then I clocked the gobby git from the pub earlier on and as our eyes met his face broke out into a grin.

"Look," he cried, "it's that knobhead who tried to get into our pub earlier on along with the rest of the Derby Fairy Cakes."

His mates burst out laughing and I immediately turned to him and yelled, "Come on then, do you want a go, or are you going to hide behind your girlfriends?"

This time it was his turn to go apeshit and I enjoyed watching the smile vanish from his ugly mug, but it was just as funny watching the reaction of the crowd. They began surging forward and waving their fists, so I stood there with my arms out egging them on and calling them all a bunch of queers.

Then one of the police officers who had been leading us around the pitch grabbed me and said, "What the fuck do you think you are doing? Keep walking, young man, and keep walking now."

I wanted to chin him. Police officer or not, nobody puts their hands on me. But I knew if I did that I would be hurled to the police station and miss the rest of the game and I didn't want that. I wanted to stay and have it out with Coventry's firm, so reluctantly did what I was told, and we marched over to where the Derby fans were situated halfway down the pitch.

The game itself did not interest me. I mean, what the hell do people see in watching a bunch of prats kicking a football round a pitch – the whole thing is ridiculous. It really is and I was so bored I spent the whole game yawning my head off or trying to wind the Coventry firm up but to no avail. They were too far away to hear me yelling at them and besides, the noise around the ground was just as loud, as both sets of fans egged their team on; I doubt even Biffo and the rest of the lads around me could hear what I was saying half the time.

I was pleased when the referee blew the final whistle and the game was over, despite the fact that Derby lost by three goals to one. Afterwards, Biffo told me that many fights between rival firms take place after the game and I was looking forward to kicking hell out of the Coventry firm but it was not to be. The police were really on the ball that day and they escorted us back to the train station and even frog marched us on to our train while keeping the Coventry mob who were trailing us and giving the big come on well back.

I was fuming we didn't manage to have a good ruck with them and said as much to Biffo but he was surprisingly philosophical about it.

"Don't worry, Harry," he said. "We did ourselves proud. We went up to Coventry and confronted their firm in their local boozer and what did they do? They locked the door and refused to come out despite having overwhelming numbers. It may mean nothing to the man on the street, but in the hooligan world that sort of thing makes you a laughing stock. Firms all around the country will piss themselves laughing at the Coventry mob when they hear about it, and they will hear about it, trust me. These things always get about, you'll see."

IPSWICH PUNISHMENT SQUAD

A few days later Derby played Ipswich Town at home. It was Wednesday 24 August 1977, and why the game was being played on a Wednesday and not on a Saturday – as was usually the case – I have no idea, but whatever the reason, I was determined to be there because Ipswich's hooligan firm, the aptly named Ipswich Punishment Squad (IPS), would be there, and I had every intention of confronting them and meting out some punishment of my own.

I arranged to meet Biffo in a pub just across the road from the baseball ground where Derby County played their home games and the first person I spotted as I approached the pub was that little kid from the other day. The one that I had knocked off his bike and booted so far in the air he had wound up crashing down onto some bins and looking somewhat bog-eyed as he did. He looked at me sheepishly, and I said to him, "What the fuck are you doing here? Want another kicking, do you?"

He just looked at me terrified and then Biffo came out the pub followed by the boy's father. The latter was spouting a corker of a black eye after the smack I had given him the other day and I said to him, "Want some more, do you?" and he just pulled back looking as terrified as his son and said, "No, Harry, I don't, and please forgive me, I didn't realise who you were the other day when I came at you with a bottle in my hand. If I had known, I wouldn't have done it. I promise you."

I said, "You're forgiven, provided you buy me and the rest of guys here a drink."

He said, "Sure, Harry. Anything you say."

We went into the pub and immediately the place fell silent and people started moving hastily out of my way.

"Is that him?" I heard one guy whisper to another in a nervous tone. "Is that Hatchet Harry?"

"Yeah, that's him," murmured another. "But for Christ's sake never upset him or you'll regret it. The guy went to my school and he's a fucking lunatic, I once saw him beat a much taller lad who had crossed him to a pulp with a knuckleduster."

At the bar, the landlady stood looking at me with an odd expression on her face. She was a middle-aged woman, with her hair tied back in a bun and winkles lining her face. I would imagine in her youth she had been quite a good-looking chick but not now. Now the ravages of time were clearly visible, and it was clear that in the looks department she was no longer the beauty she once was. Still, like I said, she was looking at me in an odd way and one which looked as though she was torn between shock and surprise at seeing me and I said to her, "What the fuck's wrong with you? Fancy me, do you?" And she just shook her head with a wary expression on her face, and said, "No, love. But seeing as everybody else in here seems to be gaping at you in awe, I thought I might as well join in."

I had to laugh at that and then turned to the guy with the black eye and said, "Mine's a pint of Guinness but you'll have to ask the other lads what they want."

Well, he looked crestfallen of course, particularly as he was hoping if he bought me a pint he would not have to buy the rest of the lads a drink, but he paid up quietly enough and handed the landlady a wad of notes which he took from a wallet he pulled out of his leather jacket before putting it in his pocket and plonking himself down on a bar stool.

I took a long gulp of my beer before putting my glass down and fixing him with an ingratiating stare.

"So who the fuck are you anyway? What's your name?"

"I'm Tommo," he said. "I'm one of the founding members of the firm. Been there from the start."

"Really," I said, taking another long gulp of my beer. "Then I take it you've been in some pretty violent clashes with rival firms over the years then."

"Oh aye," he said, his face burning with pride. "Fought the best of them, I have. Including Middlesbrough's Frontline."

"Middlesbrough Frontline."

The man took a swig of his pint and nodded. "Yeah, Middlesbrough Frontline. They think they're one of the hardest firms in the country, but we soon showed them. Took over their town we did, when we were there and confronted them outside their pub. The bastards panicked and legged it down the street despite there being over two hundred of them. Never forgot it. That happened on 5 April 1975, and the date will stay with me forever. In fact, it's a date that will stay with many of us forever because from that moment on we became one of the most feared and respected firms in the country, even Harry the Dog fears us."

"Who?"

"Harry the Dog, Millwall's top boy and a right lunatic. He's the leader of Millwall's firm the F-Troop and said to be the hardest thug in the country but I soon put him in his place. We played them in October 1970, at home, and as soon as they left the train station we confronted them. I said to Harry the Dog who was giving us the big come on, 'Fancy your chances, do you?' and knocked him out with one punch. The rest of his firm legged it back onto the train station and to this day have not been back to Derby again."

As he was talking the pub was filling up and I was aware that many of the newcomers were looking at me with a mixture of awe and fear on their faces, some of them loitering at the edge of the group I was with. One of them, a tall, freckled lad with red hair was clearly more keen than most because he kept shaking his head at everything Tommo said and then suddenly started contradicting him.

"He's talking rubbish, Harry," he said, putting his arm around Tommo and addressing me in a slightly mocking tone. "The man's never met Harry the Dog in his life, or was in the firm from the start, were you, Tommo? You just like to think you were."

Tommo, went red and I put down my glass.

"Hey, dickhead," I yelled, "when I'm having a conversation, don't ever interfere. Have I made myself clear?"

The man went as red as a beetroot, particularly as the whole pub suddenly went quiet but I wasn't finished yet. "I said, have I made myself clear?"

"Yes, Harry," he said nervously. "Quite clear."

"Good, now piss off and leave us alone because I want to hear more about the firm and Tommo is going to tell me all about it, that is, after he has bought me another pint."

Tommo gave me a look, but reluctantly got his wallet out. At first, he thought I was expecting him to buy all the other lads a drink too, because he looked at them and then me, and then back at them and asked them what they wanted, but I told him it was only me he was getting in a round for. The others could buy their own drinks and I meant it. I mean, let's face it, if they had taken another free drink from him they would have been leeching off the man, and if there is one type of person I detest, it's a leech. People who expect to have things given to them without paying for it. Still, no sooner had I taken my first gulp than the pub doors swung open and in burst the kid from earlier.

"There's a bunch of rough looking characters coming this way," he yelled, "and I'm sure they're the Ipswich firm."

I jumped up and dashed through the door with the Derby crew behind me. The kid was right, they were the Ipswich firm because the minute they clocked us, one of them waved a banner at us which said

Ipswich Punishment Squad on it before dancing around like a giant pansy and giving it the big I am.

I said, "Let's get them," before lunging at them and scattering them left, right and centre. The Ipswich lot were clearly taken by surprise and even more surprised when I laid four of them out, one after another. Then one of them pulled a knife out on me and leapt at me with it, but I darted to my left and he ended up stabbing one of his mates who had been sneaking up behind me with a bottle in his hand. The latter slumped to the deck clutching his arm where the knife had cut him but that wasn't the end of his woes. I kicked him so hard in the face he was soon seeing stars and then turned to the guy with a knife in his hand and pulled my hatchets out of my jacket, the ones I had used in Lewisham to attack the reds and which I had kept despite the fact they were not mine. The ones made of hard rubber, but which looked the real thing.

The minute the prat with the knife saw them, he screamed and fled for his life. The rest of the Ipswich Punishment Squad followed suit and I heard one of them yell to another, "Who the hell was that lunatic with the hatchets, has he escaped from the local lunatic firm or what?"

"Dunno, mate," his buddy replied. "But whoever he is he's certainly on the lunatic fringe."

I wanted to chase after them but a police siren wailed through the air and so I shot back into the pub with the rest of the Derby crew behind me. All of them were buzzing from what they had seen and were full of compliments, telling me they had never seen anything like it in the whole of their lives.

"That was fantastic," one said.

"Fucking brilliant," cried another.

"You've put them to shame, Harry."

"Never seen a rival firm been sent packing like that before."

"You're the top boy round here, mate! You're the top boy."

I slammed my glass down with such force it was a wonder it didn't smash.

"What the fuck do you think you were all playing at?" I said, with such venom they instinctively cowered back. "I've never seen anything so pathetic in all of my life. There I was, kicking the hell out of Ipswich's firm and what the fuck were you lot doing? You were just stood there looking on as though you were spectators at a show. It was fucking embarrassing to say the least."

There was a faint ripple of a protest from one or two of the lads, but I cut them short.

"Listen, you fucking idiots," I said, glaring at them angrily. "There's going to be huge changes to this firm, for one thing, I'm taking over as leader." I glanced at Biffo. "Do you have a problem with that?"

He shook his head.

"And for another, we are going to change our name."

"What to, Harry?" somebody asked meekly.

"To the Derby Lunatic Fringe," I replied. "One of those Ipswich prats referred to me as being on the lunatic fringe. Well, he's right, I am and what's more I like the tag the lunatic fringe, it's kind of catchy. So, from now on the Derby Fairy Cakes is out, and the Derby Lunatic Fringe is in, and anybody or anyone who thinks otherwise should make their objections known now."

Very wisely, nobody did.

FOREST EXECUTIVE CREW

A few days later we hit the jackpot. Derby played Nottingham Forest away and its firm, the Forest Executive Crew (FEC), were considered our biggest rivals because they were our near neighbours and years of hostility existed between the two. Indeed, Tommo told me they had fought several pitch battles with them over the years and lost everyone but not today. Today, I was confident of success and after all why not? I mean, they weren't going to be fighting a bunch of fairy cakes but the Derby Lunatic Fringe.

We got to Nottingham at about one and immediately headed towards the City Ground where Forest played their home games. Biffo told me it was customary on such occasions to send spotters out to try and locate a rival firm if we did not know where they were, or where they would be drinking but there was no need to go that far. They found us rather than we found them, or more specifically, one of their spotters did. He was stood on a corner trying to remain inconspicuous but the minute he clocked us, he scurried away and we immediately gave chase.

The City Ground was situated not far from the River Trent and it wasn't long before we found ourselves running alongside it, pushing people out of the way, and smacking anybody who dared to complain in the mouth and leaving them flat out on the deck. Football hooligans are not known for being nimble on their feet, and that is true of our firm as much as anybody else's, but the same could not be said for this guy we were chasing. This guy was like a little whippet who just seemed to get further and further away from us, no matter how hard we pushed ourselves and no matter how determined we were to get him; even Simsy, who was the fastest runner amongst us, could not catch him.

I said to Biffo, "Who the fuck are we chasing, Jessie Owens or what?" but he just laughed and said, "No, Harry, we're not, but whoever we are chasing you can't really blame him for running that fast because if I had you on my back I would be running like hell too."

We continued to chase the spotter, but it was obvious it was a waste of time and we were just thinking of packing it in when a very strange thing happened. Instead of continuing onwards towards the ground and disappearing into the crowd as any normal person would do, he suddenly turned left towards no man's land and down some steps along a long winding path towards a dark and dingy tunnel. I thought, where the fuck is he going. Is he mad or what? If I was running for my life I would not be running this way. I would be running towards the ground. Still, he hadn't, and after we had chased him down the steps, along the path and into the tunnel which was like the black hole of Calcutta, we were so knackered we had to stop to get our breath and recover our strength, particularly as the prat we were chasing had now reached the end of the tunnel and disappeared from view.

Then, we heard a lot of yelling and screaming, and when I looked up I saw a bunch of hard-looking characters (clutching baseball bats, bottles and other assorted weapons) suddenly appear at the end of the tunnel, along with the little weasel we had been chasing and I didn't need Biffo to tell me he had led us into a trap because that was obvious, even before more yobs appeared behind us blocking our retreat. I hadn't come here to retreat so it didn't bother me in the least that we had been lured into a trap, although it unsettled the rest of the lads and many of them had red faces and were shaking like a leaf but not me. I had come here to fight and fight I was going to. The only question was who was going to get it first. The prats in front of me or those goons behind me?

I said to Biffo, "Which of these morons is their leader, do you know?" and he just nodded and said, "Him, Harry, directly in front of us wearing the red shirt and clutching the baseball bat, he's their leader and a right lunatic he is too. In fact, he's one of the hardest hooligans in the country."

I said, "Lovely, I'll have him first."

So I rushed over and smashed my rubber hatchet over his head and he quickly saw stars. The guys around him were gobsmacked and all of them backed off quickly but I wasn't prepared to let it go at that and began laying into them one after another, and it wasn't long before they were hitting the deck or fleeing for their lives. Usually the latter, because when one member of a firm legs it, the chances are the rest will follow. So within a few minutes most of the goons on this side of the tunnel had legged it and those who hadn't were either on the floor writhing in agony or flat out for the count.

Then I heard the leader say, "Who the fuck are you?" and when I looked down he was clutching his head and glaring at me through bleary eyes.

"Hatchet Harry," I said, "of the Derby Lunatic Fringe."

"Who?" he said, puzzled.

"Hatchet Harry."

"Never heard of you," he replied.

I smashed him over the head with my hatchet and he slumped to the floor flat out for the count. "Well, you have now," I said, curling my lips back in a grin.

I dragged him back into the tunnel and then turned my attention to the goons at the other end of it.

"Hey, dickheads," I shouted. "Here's your leader and the rest of your firm have legged it or are out for the count. Look."

The goons took one look at their unconscious leader lying at my feet, and the others behind him and legged it. I didn't have time to yell, "Come on then, let's get to it," as I wanted to because they'd run off. So we chased them but it was a waste of time. By the time we got to the end of the tunnel, they were up the steps and by the time we got to the top of the steps they were already near their stadium and disappearing amongst the crowds, so we just stopped and shouted, "DLF, DLF, DLF," as the last of them vanished from sight altogether.

MAN UNITED'S RED ARMY

If things could not get any better, Derby's next game was Manchester United at home and I knew that its firm, the Red Army, would bring large numbers with them. Indeed, Tommo told me that they "had the hardest firm in the country and if we beat them then we could rightly call ourselves the hardest firm in the land."

I said, "We are the hardest firm in the land and after next Saturday's fracas the whole country will know about it. Man United's firm in particular."

That, however, was easier said than done. One of the problems we had was that we were quite a small firm, no more than thirty or forty at most, whereas Man United could call upon five hundred on away games and even more when playing at home. Luckily, we weren't playing them at home, instead on our own patch, but we would still be vastly outnumbered, so I called the guys to a meeting and told them that each of them had to find another five members to join the firm.

I said that if anybody objected we could discuss it in private, but as everybody knew what that meant nobody did and within days we had over a hundred new members. Lads from all over Derby who I didn't know yet knew me by reputation just accepted I was the leader of the firm which was slightly disappointing because if anybody had objected, it would have been fun smashing a hatchet over their head and showing them who was boss.

Come match day, I was buzzing as I always was. I was so excited that I didn't even spend the previous night sniffing glue, shagging prostitutes, and getting pissed in case I woke up with a hangover and was not well enough to partake in the day's events. By the time I got down to our local boozer, wearing my trademark jeans, white top, braces, green jacket and Dr Marten Boots, I was rearing to go.

After Tommo had got me a pint, we all stood round discussing today's events and how we were going to show United's firm who really was the hardest firm in the country. I say discussed it, but our plan was really very simple. Find out where the opposition were and go and kick the hell out of them or alternately wait till they came to you and then kick the hell out of them. Remember, I was no Dani Lia. A man who I freely admit was the hardest and cleverest hooligan that ever lived, even harder than me and Harry the Dog who I told you about earlier. I did not have the intelligence and patience to plan a ruck like he could.

Dani Lia, when he was the leader of Wigan Athletic's hooligan firm, the Goon Squad back in the 1970s, would come up with all sort of ingenious ways to stop a rival firm coming onto his patch and taking liberties. On one occasion in early 1979, he arranged to meet up with Rochdale's firm, the Chosen Few, at a pre-arranged venue so they could do battle there. On arrival, the Rochdale lads got the surprise of their lives. Instead of finding the Wigan firm waiting for them clutching baseball bats, knives, or some other tool to be used as a weapon, they found instead a large soup van being run by nuns and an elderly vicar with a long pointed nose and saintly face greeting them and guiding them to one of a number of folding tables that had been laid out with beer on top. Well, of course, Rochdale's firm were gobsmacked and even more gobsmacked when the vicar pulled out a card and handed it to their top boy, who discovered that the card had been sent by Dani Lia himself and simply said that *the Goon Squad were not prepared to fight the Chosen Few given they were the hardest firm around and it would be a battle they could not win. As compensation for any expense you have incurred in getting here, Dani Lia has arranged for members of the clergy to lay on a spread for you which he hopes you will enjoy.*

Very soon they were tucking into the soup and throwing back the beer like there was no tomorrow, but it was a mistake because what they did not realise was that the elderly vicar was actually Dani Lia in disguise, and the nuns were girlfriends of fellow Goon Squad members and the soup was laced with arsenic. Not enough to kill them but enough to have them spewing up everywhere and collapsing to the ground in the most ingratiating of pain, not that Dani gave a toss. He simply waited until the last of them had dropped down in agony before revealing his true identity and telling them that if they ever threatened his firm again, he would arrange for them to have their heads chopped off their necks, before getting in the van and driving away, leaving them all spewing up on the wasteland.

Still, as I said, that was the legend that was Dani Lia. He was a planner whereas I was not. My battleplan simply consisted of finding the opposition and kicking hell out of them, or waiting until the found us, and then kick the hell out of them like they did today.

I was just pointing out to Tommo that my glass was empty when in burst his son.

"They're here, Harry," he said, addressing me directly. "The Red Army are here."

We dashed outside the pub and straightaway we spotted them. Hordes of them walking up the road clutching an assortment of bottles, baseball bats, knives and in one case what looked like a huge spear of some sort. I turned to the lads and with a big grin on my face, pulled out my hatchets and said somewhat theoretically, "Showtime, boys."

Then I charged into the Red Army and began knocking them down left, right and centre. The United firm were clearly shocked by this sudden onslaught and bottles were flying from every angle through the air. I would like to think that we had the United firm on the retreat, but the fact was we didn't. Our situation was like the German position at Stalingrad, insomuch as that every time we put one of them down, ten more would appear to take their place. What was worse was that many of our own guys were dropping down like flies and others were showing signs of retreating. Then I heard Biffo's voice yell out, "There are too many of them, Harry, we should get back to the pub and regroup."

So before I knew it we were legging it back to the pub, as the United firm began jumping up and down, thinking the fight was over, and they had beat us on our home turf.

I say thinking it was all over, because trust me it wasn't. As soon as the pub doors were shut, I turned to Biffo and said, "What the fuck's going on? I thought United's firm numbered about five hundred at away games, but they've brought thousands."

He just nodded his head warily and said, "Yes, it does look that way doesn't it, Harry, but no, they're being marshalled by the General, that's their top boy. He likes to put the worst fighters up front and the hardest guys behind them. That way when they do a battle with a rival firm, the cannon fodder as he calls them provide the first line of attack, while the best fighters linger behind them and wait until the opposing firm have either tired themselves out or are bogged down before storming in and forcing the rival firm on the defensive and eventually causing them to flee as they did with us. Clever, isn't it?"

It certainly was but I was still fuming and said to him, "Why the fuck didn't you tell me this before?"

Biffo just smiled and said, "It wouldn't have made any difference if I had, Harry. You would still have just gone out and laid into them anyway."

I smiled and said, "Yeah, I suppose I would."

Still, I wasn't prepared to let it end there and neither it seemed were the Red Army. They started pounding on the pub door furiously and trying to smash the windows in but found they had been outsmarted by the landlady who had installed a big oak door which was extremely thick and which even the SAS would have a problem breaking down. Moreover, she had installed shutters on the windows and as soon as she saw us storming back in with our tails between our legs, she put the shutters up, meaning they were unable to smash the windows in either. I had to give her ten out of ten for that and said to her, "That was good thinking. Having a thick door and shutters installed."

But she just smiled warily, and said, "With you being one of my regular customers, Harry, such precautions are necessary, I assure you."

Outside the noise was getting louder and I said to Biffo, "I'm going to take half the lads out the back door and round the alleyway and hit them from behind when they're not expecting it, and as soon as they turn away from the pub and come storming at us, you hit them from the rear. That way, they'll lose control and panic."

So we carried out the plan forthwith. Luckily for us there was no way round the pub from the front because there were buildings on both sides of it, so we sneaked out the back without being observed and made our way quietly around the back alley. One of the benefits of fighting on home turf is you know the territory like the back of your hand, unlike your opponents who don't know the area all that well and are fighting on unfamiliar territory. So while United's firm were still banging on the pub door and yelling and screaming for us to come out, me, Simsy and fifty other guys were quietly making our way around the alleyway and towards their rear. (I didn't know the top boy was nicknamed the General, I should have taken that name for myself.) As soon as we got to where I wanted us to be, where the alleyway brought us onto the road about fifty yards down from the pub, I saw to my delight we were right behind United's firm.

I had it whispered down the line that we were going to sneak up behind their lines quietly, and nobody was to say or do anything until I gave the order and what happened next is the stuff of legend – the film *Legend*, that is, where Tom Hardy plays both Ronnie and Reggie Kray.

I don't know if you have ever seen the film but if you haven't, there is a scene in a pub where Ronnie and Reggie are confronted by members of a rival firm and Ronnie walks out of the pub in a rage that their rivals appear underprepared for their fight, leaving Reggie to face his opponents alone. Then while Reggie is distracting the rival mob, Ronnie sneaks back in behind them, clutching two hatchets in his hand and hovering behind them before smashing it down on one of their backs and starting the fight.

Well, gossip has it the scriptwriters got the idea for that from me, because as the United firm continued to hurl abuse at the pub, I crept quietly up behind them and stood with my hatchet above my head before smashing it down on the head of bozo in front of me, sending him crashing to the ground. In fact, he hit the deck so quickly that he didn't have time even to scream which is more than can be said for the guy who was standing next to him. He began yelling like a baby when he saw me standing there with blood dripping off my hatchet and he backed off fast, knocking people out of his way as he did. But it did him no good. I just laid into him with my hatchet before turning my attention to another member of his firm and whacking it over the miserable little runt's head.

Then Simsy and the rest of the lads began storming into them with bats, clubs, you name it. Just as fantastic was the reaction of some of the older guys. Some of our new recruits were in their thirties and they had found a dustbin full of bottles and began lobbing them over our heads into their ranks, causing even more panic and disarray than there already was. We continued to lay into the Red Army and God knows where their General was or for that matter what he looked like, but right then I heard a large cry out from behind their ranks and I knew Biffo and the rest of the firm were now laying into them from the other side.

From then on there was nothing but chaos in their ranks and the only way they could flee was left or right down the road which they did, tripping over each over in the process. I wanted to smash all of them but in particular their general so I yelled out to Biffo, "Which one is he? Which is the General?"

He glanced around before pointing to a dark-haired lout running away with his tail between his legs and looking really pissed off, which was understandable, for he knew, as did the rest of his firm, that his wasn't the toughest firm around, we were, and what a moment it was. I just stood there with my hatchets raised above my head as people all around me yelled, "There's only one Hatchet Harry, only one Hatchet Harry."

CHELSEA HEADHUNTERS

Of all the firms we ever did battle with, none of them ever disappointed me more than those prats known as the Chelsea Headhunters. This lot really were a disappointment. They professed themselves to be the crème de la crème of football hooliganism but in reality, they weren't even up there with the most non-league of firms. I put them on par with Accrington Stanley and that's being kind.

We played them away on 10th September 1977, and straightaway they made it clear they weren't interested in taking us on. They were gathered outside their pub and the minute they clocked us, legged it inside and banged the door firmly shut behind them.

I yelled at one podgy prat who was staring at us through the window with a terrified expression on his face, "What the fuck's wrong with you lot? Let's get to it."

But he just put his hands out and said, "No, Harry, we don't want any trouble. We've heard about you and the Derby Lunatic Fringe and we don't want to fight you. You're too tough for us." He paused and added sheepishly, "You are Hatchet Harry, aren't you?"

I said, "Yeah, I am. But who the fuck are you?"

"I'm Jason M," he replied. "I'm Chelsea's top boy."

"Top boy," I replied with a smirk. "And you're too scared to fight us. What the fuck are you the top boy of, a bunch of pansies?"

His face went red, as indeed did the horde of skinheads behind him and I just shook my head in disgust and turned on my feet.

"Wankers," I cried, storming off down the road. "Absolute wankers."

TOP BOY

That altercation or none altercation with Chelsea's so-called firm left me absolutely fuming but not for long. As usual Biffo was able to see the good in it and pointed out that if Chelsea's firm was so terrified of fighting us and me in particular, then our reputation must have travelled far and wide and we were already being acknowledged by firms up and down the country as the hardest firm around, with me as the nation's top boy.

Of course, football violence wasn't the only thing I was involved in. Living on the dole meant I had all the time in the world to pursue my hooligan activity but the money the state gave you for doing nothing was pitiably low. In fact, once I had given my mum money for housekeeping, I had next to nothing, yet it was her who came to my rescue.

I told you before that when she was young she had worked as a prostitute and was known unflatteringly as Bouncing Barbara; well, it turned out she hadn't left the business for good. No, I'm not saying she was selling her body for cash because she wasn't, but she was providing sex for clients through the massage parlour on the shopping complex on our estate.

I was gobsmacked when she told me, because I had no idea she had a link in the business. I knew the parlour was a front for a brothel, of course, because I had used it myself on many occasions but all the same I had no idea Mum was a silent partner in the business.

I said to her, "Why didn't you tell me you had a stake in the parlour?"

And she said, "If I told you, Harry, it would have been all over the estate and that was the last thing I wanted, so I told nobody other than your father and a select few and that's why I kept it from you."

I just smiled, and said to her, "So why are you telling me now?"

She said, "Because some organisation are harassing us for protection money, Harry, so I want you and your firm to have a word in their ear."

I said, "What's in it for me?"

She smiled and said, "Money of course, along with the cheap board and lodging you already get."

I said, "Lovely, leave it with me."

A few days later these dickheads turned up at the parlour demanding money and threatening to burn the place down if they didn't get it. There were six of them in total, a small weedy-looking man in his fifties, wearing a smart suit and doing all the talking, and five tough-looking geezers stood behind him holding coshes and patting them menacingly in their hands. The girl at reception said, "Certainly, sir, our public relations consultant has your money. Please follow me."

Well, of course they were surprised by that, and the small weedy guy said, "Public relations consultant, I didn't realise this place had one."

And the girl said, "Oh yes, he's just through here," and threw open a door where they stepped out and found themselves in a huge back yard with a door at the end and me standing in the centre clutching my hatchets with blood pouring off them and my lips curled back in a grin.

Upon seeing me, the weedy guy in the suit screamed and tried to run back in the direction he came from, but the girl slammed the door shut firmly behind her, meaning he was trapped like a rabbit in the hole. Then I got to work. Without warning I smashed my hatchet down on one of his henchmen's skulls so hard that his eyes nearly popped out of his head and he dropped to his knees with blood gushing out of his skull. I wasn't finished yet. I whacked him again and again and again and he let out an almighty wail before hitting the deck and lying there flat out cold.

Then I turned to the other so-called hardmen and began battering them all over. I hit them so hard they quickly fell to the ground and then just continued to whack them until blood was pouring out of them and they were crying like babies. None of them tried to fight back which to me was incredible and all five were whimpering and begging for mercy. It was a waste of time on their part. They were pleading to the wrong man. I don't do mercy. Hurting people is something I like doing and will go out of my way to do. After all, that is why I am a football hooligan. I kept going until they were splattered all over the floor, and whimpering no more.

Then I stood up and very slowly turned to face the weedy git in the suit. This man was whimpering and cawing at the door, desperately hoping somebody would open it and let him out but there wasn't a chance in hell that that wouldn happen. The girls who worked there had been instructed that under no circumstances were they to open the back door unless they heard my voice telling them to, no matter how much screaming they heard, and anyway, the girl who had escorted them through the building was on the other side polishing her nails and making sure nobody opened the door. Of course, it's possible that this bloke was hoping a punter would open it, as the place was a brothel – er, sorry, massage parlour – but even then he was out of luck. There weren't any punters in tonight as all of them had been turned away at the door and told it would be closed until tomorrow as a water pipe had burst and needed fixing, so there was nobody to come to his rescue and he was quite alone with me.

I turned to him slowly and the minute I did, he stopped banging on the door and moved his head to face me. I don't know whether he could feel my eyes boring into him or whether it was because everything had gone quiet but that's what he did and the minute he saw me clutching my hatchets with blood on them and my lips curled into a sinister grin, the man screamed and then slid down the door and lay there in a huddle with his head tilted to one side.

I had never seen anything like it in my life and for a moment I was so taken back I just stared at him. I thought, what the fuck is wrong with him? Has he fainted? The truth was he had passed out but probably wished he hadn't because when he came to he was hanging upside down by a rope attached to a pulley above and finding himself in a right pickle.

The moment he realised where he was and that he was strung up like carcass in a butcher's shop, he began screaming and begging for mercy.

"It's okay," I said to him. "I'm not going to chop you up with my hatchets, I'm not even holding them. Right now, one of the girls inside is washing the blood off them and she wouldn't be doing that if I intended use them on you, would I? After all, what would be the point? I would only have to wash the blood off them *again* if I did, wouldn't I?"

He seemed to relax after that and even engaged in polite conversation. "No, no, mate," he said, "I don't think you would. My name is Michael by the way, who are you?"

"Harry," I said, holding out my hand, "it's nice to meet you."

He didn't shake it of course, not because he was being rude, but because he had his hands tied behind his back which meant he was unable to do so. So I didn't take offence. Instead I asked him to tell me about himself which he did. In fact, once he began talking I couldn't shut him up and he told me everything I wanted to know. Who he was, where he came from. How did he get involved in the protection business? How many in the firm were there? Who was his boss, everything, and it was a fascinating tale.

It turned out that this little weasel was the boss, and his heavies was his nephews who lived on the other side of town and who hit on the idea of running a protection racket as a way of bringing in the dosh. So far they had manged to persuade a few Paki shops to pay up or suffer the consequences of their actions. It was fascinating stuff, particularly when he told me that the reason he had targeted the massage parlour was because he was expanding his business and had seen the massage parlour as a means of doing that, but I couldn't just accept who he was because that's who he said he was. For all I know the man may have been lying and trying to pull a fast one over me. So, I relieved him of his wallet, and the huge wad of notes contained within it, before examining his driving license and taking down his name and address.

After that, I simply pocketed the cash the rest of the goons were carrying on them, before turning back to Michael and thanking him for his honesty.

"So you're not going to hit me with your hatchets then?" he said nervously.

I smiled. "Certainly not. I promised you I wouldn't, didn't I?"

"You did, you did, and I'm very grateful you're going to keep your word. Thank you, thank you," he cried.

"You're very welcome," I replied, before picking up a baseball bat and smashing the thing down in his face where I believe he screamed even louder than before.

WENDY'S MASSAGE PARLOUR

That goon and his henchmen spent the next few weeks in intensive care and I could not have cared less if they had lived or died. Neither was I concerned that they would rat on me to the police but then why should I? These bastards had turned up at the parlour demanding money with a menace and how could they explain that to the police without dropping themselves in it? In fact, I knew they wouldn't particularly as I told them that if they did I would arrange for their kids and wives to join them in intensive care and they were wise enough to know I wasn't kidding.

So I never heard from them again and life at the parlour returned to normal. I say normal but with one major exception. My mum was concerned that other low lifes might try to muscle in on the business, so she offered me the job as security guard working alongside Fat Jimmy who had provided security for the parlour for years and was quite a character in his own right. In fact, his daughter Lucy had been Mum's best friend at school and even though she emigrated to New Zealand when she was 18, she still kept in touch with Mum and Christmas cards were swapped every year. I used to say to him, "what was Mum like when she was a kid?" and he used to tell me all the skulduggery she used to get up to when she was a teenager, she and Lucy, and I used to love hearing about it. I used to say to my mum, "did you and Lucy really get up to this and that?" and she would just laugh and say, "we sure did, Harry. Happy days!"

It wasn't just fun working for Fat Jimmy (so-called because of his vast weight and roly poly appearance) it was easy, because the job was cushy, and Jimmy knew how to handle clients better than anybody. Most of the clients would come, get the service they required and pay up without any fuss, but there was always one or two who would try and get away without handing over any money and when they did Jimmy would spring into action and have a quiet word in their ear. Normally that would be enough to get them to cough up but if it wasn't Jimmy would find other ways to get the cash. Ways I would never dream of. I would've just taken them to the back yard and given them a right kicking, but Jimmy said that was the very last thing we should do.

"Remember, Harry," he said, "many of these people are professionals. Law abiding citizens with good jobs. You beat them up or assault them in any way, and quick as a flash they go running to the police and we'll be shut down quicker than you can say hey presto."

I said, "What the fuck do we do then?"

"Let them have the goods without paying." And he just laughed and said, "No, Harry, we use our brains, that's what we do."

He would come up with all sorts of ways to get the clients to pay up and I must admit they were rather clever. One of them was to say to a client, "You don't want to pay for the service you have just received, not a problem. We'll send the bill to your wife or employer along with all the little extras you've had here." That usually did the trick.

Another was to wait until he got to the car and have a hooker approach him and plant a kiss on his cheek while Fat Jimmy took a picture of it. Then the client would be informed that the picture would be sent to the press, if he didn't pay up, and it would be up to him to explain to his wife and friends what he was doing in a car park consorting with a prostitute. Sneaky. It was ingenious and once again that forced them to pay up, especially as the client was charged another ten pounds to pay for the expense of having a picture taken and for the girl's time.

But the one that really got clients rushing to pay up was to simply tell them that the girl in the photo was under 16 and if he didn't pay up everybody would think he was a nonce, particularly when the picture appeared in the local newspaper and the world and his wife saw it. Indeed, so effective was the latter, that clients would often pay more than their bill just to get on our good side and keep the photo out of the local paper, but Jimmy always refused to take any more money other than what the client owed.

"Remember, Harry," he once told me after a pretty obnoxious client had paid up and gone, "we're not here to rob them, just ensure that they pay for the service they receive."

Working at the parlour was certainly an eye opener and Jimmy taught me a lot of things about the security business and how to handle situations without employing your boots and fists, but the best thing about the job was the perks. Most of the time I just sat in the back office watching television or having a doze on the settee and keeping a low profile. Remember, it was the girls the clients came to see, not me or Jimmy; our job was simply to provide security and that was it. My absolute favourite part was getting to a massage once a day along with sex with one of the girls. My mum said it helped me understand the nature of the business but that was a load of old tosh. The real reason was because she knew I had a very violent streak in me and this was her way of keeping that violent streak under control while I was at work and what a way to go about it, providing me with sex and a massage. I mean, how many employers would do that?

So for the next few months, life for me was really good. I had a good job, was earning good dough and had the weekends off. Indeed, having the weekends off was a godsend because it allowed me to pursue my hooligan activities and satisfy my need for violence. That too was a shrewd move on my mother's part. She knew the urge to beat somebody up was just so ingrained in me that if I couldn't kick somebody's teeth in outside the parlour then sooner or later I would do it at work. Over the next few weeks we had run ins with the Leeds Service Crew who I didn't rate, Liverpool's Runcorn Riot Squad who I did, and Middlesbrough's Frontline who quite frankly bottled it and ran for their lives the minute they saw me walking towards them with a hatchet in my hand and my lips curled back in a grin.

Then we hit the jackpot again when we played Wolves away and came up against another local rival, the Wolves Subway Army. This firm had been making quite a name for itself in hooligan circles, and their leader, a rather obnoxious individual called Gilly (or Silly as we called him), was boasting they were the hardest firm around and were going to cause us great injury. It was all bullshit. The minute they saw us coming they legged it and I mean legged it. I don't know if you have ever seen a group of men running for their lives but if you haven't then trust me it's a pretty poor show. Still, years later when Gilly decided to write his autobiography he must have remembered our altercation because he decided to call his book *Running With a Pack of Wolves*, which is precisely what he did the minute he saw me coming towards him with a hatchet in my hand, and my lips curled back in a grin. He ran with a pack of wolves.

THE FIRST BLUE LETTER

The summer of 1978 began well for me. In fact, I would go so far as to say it was the best summer of my life. I had a good job, was earning good money, and was boss of the hardest firm in the country. Not only that but my reputation had spread so far and wide that many hooligans – and not just those in my own firm – were calling me the daddy of British hooliganism and were talking about me in pubs and clubs up and down the country. I had become so infamous that the *Hooligan News* got in touch and even did an exposé on me. Incredible isn't it, that football hooligans should have their own newspaper and trust me, you will not find it in any shop, supermarket or newsagent as it is produced underground and sold mostly in pubs, boxing venues and football matches but nonetheless, football hooligans love it and anyone who is everyone in the hooligan world has been in it at some stage. Indeed, there is a well-known adage in the hooligan world that if you've never been in the *Hooligan News* then you are probably a nobody on the hooligan scene, and in a world where reputation means everything, it's not the least bit surprising that hooligans would do almost anything to get their picture in the paper.

That wasn't the only reason why that summer of 1978 was a good one for me. It was the first and only time I travelled abroad for my holiday. That came about because the landlady of my local boozer, you know, the middle-aged tart who just stared at me when we first met and I asked her what the fuck she was staring at and whether she fancied me, just shook her head and said, "no, love, but seeing as everybody else in here seems to be gaping at you in awe, I thought I might as well join in," well, it was her who suggested I book a holiday and go and have fun abroad for a couple of weeks because she said everybody needs to relax and chill out for a bit, and I suppose when you think about it she had a point.

Indeed, Monica was a bit of an enigma to me. Over the weeks I had come to know her well and she wasn't really a tart. In fact, she never had sex with anybody despite me and others trying it on with her a couple of times and when I asked her why not, she just said that there was a man in the past who she loved, but he was taken from her tragically and he could never be replaced by anyone, not even me.

I had to give her ten out of ten for that because grief can affect people in different ways as I well knew because only a month earlier, my beloved grandfather, Eddy Hatchett had died, and his death hit me hard. Iit hit a lot of people hard, including my parents and grandmother but it was Monica who helped me come to terms with the grief. I used to sit by the bar and drone on and on about what a great man he was, how he had been Oswald Mosley's bodyguard before the war, and how he had beaten the best street fighters of the day. I told her everything and really opened my heart to her, particularly when my grandmother died of a broken heart shortly afterwards. I had never opened my heart to anybody before, not even my parents, but she had a way about her which made you want to pour your heart out to her.

I was glad Monica persuaded me take a holiday in the sun and so that July, me, Simsy, Biffo and a few others booked a holiday in Tenerife. Tenerife was chosen because we heard it was good for pulling the birds and partying and that was just what I needed, a holiday away from it all with nothing but booze, women and sunny beaches for a full fortnight.

Mind you we got off to a bad start. I hadn't realised I was terrified of flying until the minute I saw the plane standing on the tarmac. My face went as white as chalk. I don't know why because I knew I would be flying and up till then it hadn't been a problem but once I saw the plane all that changed. My arm hair virtually stood up on its own and inside I felt sort of queer. I said to Biffo, "I can't go. I don't feel well," but he just said, "don't worry, Harry. It's pre-flight nerves. A lot of people have them."

Well, whether it was, or it wasn't, I was bloody terrified and as the plane left the tarmac and rose high up into the air, I couldn't look and buried my head in my arms and refused to talk to anybody. I didn't bother to have the meal when the stewardess came round dishing up food. Simsy tried to made a joke of it and said, "Harry, if the plane crashes, it's only because it was the pilot's time who was up, not yours," but I told him if he didn't shut it and leave me alone, his time would be up whether or not the plane crashed.

Once we landed and my feet were firmly on the ground, I was quite myself again and we sailed through customs without a hitch. Because we had booked with Thomas Cook, one of their reps was waiting for us who escorted us to a coach, which in turn took us to our hotel and I must admit the place wasn't bad. In fact, it was quite good. We had apartments on the ground floor next to the swimming pool and they were lavishly sparse with a large bedroom, fridge, safe, and en-suite bathroom. I know some people end up in some hellholes when they go away but I wasn't one of them and I was very pleased with the accommodation we got.

Even better, the beach was only a short distance away and we spent the first week lying on it building up our suntans, swimming in the sea and partying till the early hours of the night. Tenerife is known for its partying and oh boy did we party. Sometimes we partied that hard than on one occasion I ended up waking up on the beach, although how I got there and didn't freeze to death in the early hours is anybody's guess. I didn't get into any fights either, which I'm sure you will agree is a miracle for me, but that could not be said for the second week.

The second week was like holidaying in the O.K. Corral with fights breaking out everywhere. It's an odd thing but even the weediest little toe rag when high on booze thinks he is Superman and starts lashing out at anyone he thinks is staring at him funny or just in his way but unluckily for one weedy git with a Scottish accent, that person was me.

I was just standing by the bar waiting to get served when he started pushing people out the way while clearly the worst for wear. I turned to see what all the fuss was about and he clocked me before pointing a bony finger at me and yelling, "Hey you, Jimmy. Get out ma fucking way." I told him to piss off and he lashed out at me. So I punched him and he wheeled back and hit the deck, dragging some unfortunate souls he had been standing next to down with him.

Then his girlfriend went berserk and started lashing out at me. She was a weedy looking thing too and I think she thought that being a girl, I would not hit back but that wasn't in my nature. Hit me, and I will hit you back. She hit me and so I smacked her in the face and she fell back and ended up seeing stars. Some of the locals weren't too pleased and started mumbling amongst themselves, so I told them to shut it or they would get ot too.

Then my eyes nearly popped out my head. Some little thing in a mini skirt pushed her way through the crowd saying she was a nurse and knelt down by those jerks and began taking their pulses to see if they were all right. At least that's what I thought she was doing. But then another fight broke out further up the bar and as everybody dashed over to see what was going on, I watched her take the purse out of the girl's jacket, before turning to theboyfriend and removing his wallet from his trousers.

Then she noticed me staring at her, and her face went as red as a beetroot, but I wasn't disgusted by her behaviour. On the contrary it quite amused me but I didn't let on. Instead I told her she was a thief and I was taking her to the police station.

"No, no," she cried, in a cockney accent. "Please don't. They'll lock me up and put me in prison."

"Should have thought about that, shouldn't you," I replied sternly. "Before you decided to rob them."

"Well, what's wrong with that?" she cried, fixing me with a stern expression. "You beat them up. I just took advantage of the fact."

I had to laugh at her cheek and because she was a good-looking chick, I gave her an ultimatum.

"Look," I said, eyeing her up and down, "I won't take you to the police station if you sleep with me, how's that?"

She stared at me with an incredulous expression on her face, and her eyes had gone all hard and serious, before murmuring, "You what?"

I said, "Sleep with me and I won't call the police. The choice is yours."

"But ... but that's rape," she stammered.

I smiled. "Well, it's either that or it's off to the police station for you and trust me, you won't like it. You will hate it. Getting arrested here is not like it is back in the UK. You don't just get charged and told to appear in court at a later date. You get thrown in jail and have to wait months until your case comes up. Even years. And you won't like the people you're inside with. Some of them may rape you. So you might as well let me do it. Who knows, you might enjoy it."

She continued to stare at me and I could see she didn't really want to have sex with me, so I wasn't surprised when she turned on her feet and did a runner. I thought about chasing after her but decided against it, because just then two Spanish chicks walked past me, and I could see by the way they looked at me that they were up for it and fancied the pants off me. I was up for it too and quickly left them in no doubt of it, but the only problem was deciding which of them to have, because they were both giving me the come on. So in the end I decided to have them both and bloody good fun it was. During the last week I spent my time shagging my way through the local talent and by the time I landed in England I felt great, relaxed and full of the joys of spring. Even the flight home hadn't daunted my spirits, even though I had been dreading it.

Mum and Dad were in good spirits when I got home, and I discovered that it was because some Anti-Nazi League scumbag had been killed protesting against the NF in London. Mum was so pleased that the next morning when I woke up she brought me breakfast in bed along with the morning paper with a picture of the red who had been killed on the front page.

"Oh, Harry," she said, almost as an afterthought with her hand on the door, "a letter came from you when you were on holiday."

"A letter?" I said, puzzled.

She handed me a blue envelope.

I tossed it to one side and consumed my breakfast before grabbing the paper and reading its contents. Apart from the dead anti-fascist prick, there was nothing of interest, so I threw it side and went for a shower. The water was steaming hot and by the time I came out and made my way back to the bedroom, I was feeling clean, well fed and full of the joys of spring. Plonking myself on my bed, I noticed the blue envelope and casually tore it open. Inside was a picture and as I stared at it the full horror of what I was staring at hit me full on in the face. For what I was staring at was a picture of me lobbing the brick at that dork who I had killed on my first day of secondary school along with the word 'murderer' written in blood on the back of it in big bold words.

PORK SANDWICH

To say I was gobsmacked would be an understatement. I was more than just that, I was dumbstruck. Various thoughts flicked through my mind. Like who had taken the picture and why. And why had they not shown it to the police and why were they sending it to me now.

The last two were a particular worry but I thought I knew the answer to them. Blackmail, it must be. Why else would somebody send the picture to me and not the police, unless they were hoping to make a fast buck out of me, and they had chosen their time well, hadn't they. What with raking it in from the parlour, I was ripe for the picking.

Nobody blackmails me and I swore when I got my hands on the scumbag responsible, they would get it. The only problem was I didn't have a clue who had sent it. There was nothing in the letter to suggest who the writer was. Well, photo sender I should say because there was nothing in the envelope but that photograph of me and that in itself was quite creepy. You would have thought there would have been a note of some description, but no, there was nothing, except the word murderer written and that wa scary. It suggested a calculated mind rather than a violent one and one who knew how to create an aura of menace without writing anything other than a single word.

That said, it didn't mean I didn't examine the letter in order to find some clue as to the sender's identity. You may not believe this but although I was not academically minded, I was quite a prolific reader. My room was full of books on Hitler and the Nazis but also on murder. In fact, I had more books on murder than I had on Hitler and remember, he was my hero. I can't quite explain why murder fascinated me so much, except to say that it usually involved excessive violence of some description which I found appealing. Whatever the reason for my macabre fascination on the subject, I had many books on real life murderers like George Joseph Smith, the brides in the bath murderer, Dr Crippen or Ian Brady, who I would willingly have strung up along with all the other nonces out there.

I even had books written by famous authors like Agatha Christie, Edgar Allan Poe and Dorothy L. Sayers, all famous for their murder mysteries and bloody good yarns they were too. Well, Agatha Christie's were anyway, some of the ones by Edgar Allan Poe were a bit boring and Dorothy L. Sayers titles were a great cure for insomnia. The best were the Sherlock Holmes mysteries penned by Arthur Conan Doyle. What I particularly liked about these were the way he could deduce somebody's age, gender and social status simply by studying an object or letter thoroughly. I'm not going to go through the methods he used because you can buy his books and read them yourself, but when I tell you that I examined that letter to me very thoroughly, that is exactly what I did, by employing the methods outlined in Conan Doyle's books.

And what did I deduce you may well ask?

Well one, that the letter came from Coventry, because it had a Coventry post mark. Two, it was sent two days earlier, because it was stamped on that date, and three, the sender was well-educated as the writing was neat and displayed a certain amount of intelligence.

That didn't get me very far. That could apply to many people but alas, not to many people of my acquaintance. But then let's face it, football hooliganism is not a pastime that tends to attract the well-educated and intelligent and for obvious reasons. There are exceptions of course. Dani Lia for example had a formidable intellect and was top of his class at school, but he was the exception rather than the rule. Most football hooligans are brainless morons who couldn't plan a piss up in a brewery, which you will discover if you have read their autobiographies that are filling bookstores at the moment.

I was rattled, and it takes a lot to rattle me but if that picture found its way to the police, I would be doing some serious jail time for murder. So I quickly tore the picture up and burnt it in the ashtray and then flushed the burnt remains down the loo so nobody could use it against me and prayed that whoever had sent it had not made copies, despite having the rather uncomfortable feeling that they had.

For the next few days I went round in a strop, lashing out at anybody for anything. I even lashed out at Monica when she asked me to calm down, which led her to throw me out of the pub and bar me for a week until I had learned some manners. The first time I had been thrown out of any place and which raised a few eyebrows, not to mention a few laughs.

It was annoying. I couldn't talk about the letter, because then people would want to know what was in it, and I couldn't tell them that without telling them about the photo and hence the murder, so I spent a lot of my time when I was not working at the massage parlour attending NF demonstrations and fighting with Pakis, lefties and other unwashed scum and it was a great way to unwind I can tell you. Not as great as kicking hell out of some rival firm, because they were up for a ruck and came all tooled up, whereas the anti-fascist scum were there to hold what they called a democratic protest, and yell "Nazi scum of our streets," but it was still fun beating the hell out of them.

On one occasion I nutted this red bitch in the face who came over and tried giving it the big I am, sending her crashing to the ground with blood pouring down her face. On another I punched this long-haired hippy so hard he virtually flew through the air and ended up seeing stars for a week. The best though was when we were making our way home from a protest and saw these Pakis who we had seen at the demonstration earlier on giving us abuse and yelling "come on then" from the safety of police lines.

I said to the bus driver, "Quick, stop the bus" and we jumped out and began chasing them down the street. It was hilarious when they saw us hurling towards them and they yelled out in terror, and it was even more hilarious when they split up and one ended up running down a one-way street and we cornered him as he cowered against a wall.

But the best bit is what happened next. Because this Paki was no more than 12 or 13, I took out this pork sandwich I had bought at a shop earlier on and asked the kid if he was a Muslim.

He nodded, too scared to speak.

"I said, are you a fucking Muslim?" Raising my voice to a scream.

"Yes," he cried, with his arms covering his face as though he was bracing himself for a beating.

"Good," I said. "Eat this." I handed him the pork sandwich.

The kid grabbed it nervously and stared at it with a look of alarm on his face.

"Go on," I said encouragingly but with a hint of menace in my voice. "Eat it. There's a good boy."

The kid looked at me with a look of pure alarm on his face.

"But … but I can't," he said tearfully in a Paki accent. "Eating pork is against my religion. I cannot do this."

I took a menacing step towards him.

"Eat it, you little Paki or I'll ram it down your throat."

I pulled out my hatchets and stood there hovering over him.

The kid burst into tears, but I wasn't having any of it. In my eyes, crying is just a delaying tactic. Something people often do when they are told to do something but don't want to do it.

So I yelled, "That's it," and swung my hatchet above my head and he yelled out in terror before gulping his sandwich down which would not have pleased Ganesha, Buddha or whatever they called their god.

MAN CITY'S BLAZING CREW

The start of the 1978-1979 football season took place on 19 August 1978, and I was delighted we were playing Manchester City at home. It wasn't just because the city's firm, the Blazing Crew, were rated one of the best in the country, it was because its members included a bunch of niggers who called themselves the Cool Cats and as you know I can't stand niggers or anybody else who isn't part of the master race. So I was looking forward to meeting these race mixers and introducing them to my hatchets because let's face it, any firm that allows niggers into its ranks deserves nothing more than to have a hatchet smashed over their miserable heads.

The day was a disappointment because the City firm did not show for reasons I still don't know to this day but that could not be said for when we played them at home on 10 November 1978.

We waited for them at the train station and as soon as they emerged, they started to give us the big come on and yelling all sorts of abuse at us so I moved forward and shouted at them, "Well, come on then, stop talking and let's get to it," but it was a waste of time because the police were out in large numbers and we couldn't get anywhere near them.

Well, not outside the ground anyway. Inside it was completely different. The game was quite a good one and the fans were egging on their respective teams when for no apparent reason the referee stopped the game.

I didn't know what was going on and neither, it seemed, did anybody in the stadium and very soon somebody yelled, "Why are we waiting?" Then somebody else repeated the question, and before I knew it the whole ground was singing, "Why are we waiting? Why are we waiting?", Man city fans included.

But then somebody shouted out, "Shut it everyone, some old guy's had a heart attack."

"Heart attack?" cried another.

"Heart attack," said the first voice. "Look!"

We all looked and saw a bunch of medics carrying a stretcher across the ground.

"For fuck's sake," somebody said. "It's true."

"Well, that's it then, the match is bound to be called off," said another voice.

Then I heard a lot of yelling behind me and very soon a group of vicious-looking thugs were laying into our lads from behind.

"What the fuck's going on?" I said.

"It's City's firm," said a voice on my right. "They've sneaked up behind us while we were watching the commotion on the pitch and laying into our rear."

"What," I yelled, getting my hatchets out my jacket. "Let's get them."

That was easier said than done, however. The attack had taken us so much by surprise that most of our mob who had been stood at the back had found themselves being whacked on the head by an assortment of clubs, bottles and sticks and had hit the deck before anybody knew what was happening, and the rest were in retreat, jumping over seats and walls to get away.

In fact, the whole thing quickly became a rout (because as I have said before, when one person turns to run, others do too) and within moments people were yelling and screaming as City's firm continued to lay into our rear guard, causing us to fall back and spill out onto the pitch.

I say us but there were tons of ordinary fans spilling out onto the pitch because City's firm were attacking us and them with equal measure. That was hardly surprising because hooligans don't go round with the word hooligan written on them. Neither do they have a uniform which makes it clear they are a member of any hooligan firm. What they tend to do is dress and look like everybody else so it's not really shocking that even the very old as well as the very young sometimes end up getting clobbered (as I knew only too well as I had done a lot of the clobbering myself).

Indeed, the City firm were like a bunch of wild animals just lashing out at all and sundry. I saw one of them smack an elderly lady in the face, who was just stood there unable to believe what was going on behind her. Her husband got a punch too, a frail-looking bloke wearing a flat cap who looked as though he was in his eighties.

A young woman in her twenties received a punch, and her boyfriend too, a weedy-looking nerd who was trembling with fear and looked as though he was going to burst out crying.

Then I saw a bunch of niggers coming running towards us from the other side of the pitch and I said to one of our firm, "Who the fuck is this – the Zulus?"

"No, Harry," he cried, "I think they're the Cool Cats – City's black firm. The reason they stayed over there while their white buddies sneaked up on us from behind is because we would have spotted them a mile of if they did, what with them being niggers and all that."

Well, that was true but the sight of niggers invading our home pitch incensed me just as much as the thousands of ordinary fans around the ground and before I knew it, they were chasing the Cool Cats who were unaware of the commotion behind them and heading towards us like a horde of rampaging Zulus.

Then they steamed into us and I have to admit they were a pretty tasty crew with their fists sending a lot of my firm tumbling down to the ground. I too was knocked to the ground but quickly jumped to my feet and began laying into them with a ferocity that took them by surprise and caused one or two of them to hit the ground and remain there, out for the count.

I didn't get any further, though. By now the Derby fans behind them had caught up with them and were laying into them with such overwhelming numbers the niggers were dropping like flies, and once their white counterparts behind us saw what was happening, they began backing off slowly before legging it the way they came, but their way was blocked on all sides by Derby fans, many of whom were now attacking City's firm as me and the rest of the Derby

Lunatic Fringe just stood there shouting, "DLF, DLF," as once again we defeated another top firm on our home turf.

EVERTON

If there is one group of people I hate just as much as Pakis, niggers and queers, it's Scousers. That is, the brainless morons who hail from the hellhole known as Liverpool, on the North West coast, and are so full of crap that every time they open their mouth nothing but lies come out of it.

A good example of which can be found in Andy Nicholls's book, *Scally: Confessions of a Category C Football Hooligan.* I mean really. In it he gives the impression that Everton's firm, the Country Road Cutters, were one of the hardest in the country and feared nobody, and took on all challengers and won but the truth was very different. They, like Chelsea, were another firm who were all hype and no action as events on 26 August 1978 showed.

We travelled up by train and as soon as we came out the station, we saw the usual hordes of police officers waiting to escort us and the rest of the Derby fans up to the ground. That didn't surprise me; what did surprise me was the reaction we got from the Everton fans. They spotted us as we got near their ground and I thought, oh good, party time but instead of just streaming into us as any self-respecting firm would have done, they began clapping and taking photos of us.

I said to Biffo, "What the fuck's going on? What are they clapping for?"

But he didn't know, and we just stood looking on gobsmacked as the County Road Cutters continued to clap and take our pictures. Even the police were looking on in amazement and more than one or two were scratching their heads in bewilderment. I swear to God, I have never seen anything like it in my life.

What made it even more bizarre was it wasn't just Everton's hooligan element that was clapping and taking our pictures, but hordes of ordinary fans as well, including – I'm pleased to say – throngs of girls, aged between 16 and 19 who were hurled together in groups and began jumping up and down screaming when they spotted us as though we were the Beatles visiting the city.

Then I heard one of them yell, "Which of them is he? Which of them is the infamous Hatchet Harry?"

And then another female voice cried out, "Yeah. Which of them is he? Which of them is the famous Hatchet Harry we've been hearing about?"

I glanced at Biffo with a look of utter disbelief on my face but he was even more astounded than I was, in fact he was so shocked he had to pinch himself just to make sure he wasn't dreaming.

I did likewise but before the police could move us on, some girl clad in an Everton scarf and blue hat came running over yelling, "Hatchet Harry, Hatchet Harry, can I have your autograph? I think you're so cool."

Well, what could I say but yes, and I signed a copy of the *Hooligan News* she was holding. Then another girl shot forward, followed by another and another. I was surrounded by hordes of teenage girls begging for my autograph and planting kisses on my cheek.

I heard Biffo say to one of them. "What's going on, love? Why all this interest in Harry?"

And she said, "Haven't you heard? He's in the *Hooligan News* again. Look."

She handed him a copy and as I glanced over his shoulder, my eyes nearly popped out of my head. For on the front cover there was a picture of me on a street in the dead of night clutching a hatchet with blood dripping off it. The very same picture that is on the front cover of this book actually.

I said to Biffo, "Where the fuck did they get that from? That picture was taken a couple of weeks back outside my local boozer as part of a drunken prank."

But he just shook his head and said, "I haven't got a clue, mate. I didn't even know you had posed for the camera."

It turned out that wasn't the only picture of me in the *Hooligan News*. On pages two and three they had a section headed *Hatchet Harry in action*, and there were pictures of me at just about every football fight I had been in, including one of me streaming into the Ipswich firm with my boots and fists, sending them fleeing for their lives.

There was also a picture of me stood outside the favourite pub of the Chelsea Headhunters, as its members hid inside, and another of me chasing after Notts Forest hooligans with a hatchet in my hand, and even one of me attacking members of the Man City's Blazing Crew as they cowered in fear.

The best one was of me with Man United hooligans with a hatchet above my head and my lips curled back in a grin, as I stood behind them, posed to smash it down on one of their unsuspecting skulls.

I said to Biffo, "Where the fuck did they get their hands on that picture, or for that matter, every other picture in here?"

He said, "Dunno, Harry, but that's journalists for you. They'll find information on anybody if they are so inclined."

I wasn't complaining, I was lapping up the attention and adulation I was getting from all these beautiful Scouse girls. I mean, the whole thing was rather ridiculous. Not only were they throwing their arms around me and plonking sloppy kisses on my handsome mush, they were also asking me to sign their shirts and posing for pictures with me like I was some famous Hollywood star.

Just when I was thinking things just couldn't get any more bizarre, this skinhead came up clad in an Everton shirt and extending his hand.

"Harry," he cried, shaking my hand warmly and posing for a camera shot. "Great to meet you. I've been so looking forward to this meeting."

"Why?" I replied. "Who the fuck are you anyway?"

"I'm your opposite number at Everton," he replied, puffing out his chest with pride.

"My opposite number?" I said, puzzled.

"Yeah," he said, breathing beer fumes over me as he did. "I'm top boy at Everton. I lead the Country Road Cutters."

I said, "You lead them?"

"Yeah," he cried, "I–"

"You lead them?" I yelled, pushing the girls away and reaching inside my jacket for my hatchets.

The man's eyes nearly popped out of his head when he saw them and immediately burst out in explanation.

"No, no, Harry, you don't understand. I haven't come here to fight you, I've come here to honour you, and not just me but the rest of my firm and everybody else here. You're the hardest hooligan in the country, everybody knows it and we've come to pay our respects to you. So please can I have some pictures with you? It would be something to show the grandkids when I grow old."

BIRMINGHAM CITY ZULUS

I may have been gaining cult status amongst some sections of the hooligan fraternity but there was no way I was going to let that prevent me from laying into my rivals whenever I came across them as Birmingham City's firm the Zulus was about to find out.

We were playing them at home the following Saturday and I couldn't wait to stream into them because they were probably the most anti-fascist outfit in the country and their ranks were full of niggers, in fact they had so many niggers that this was the reason they called themselves the Zulus and they behaved like the Zulus too.

We had agreed to meet them on wasteland on the edge of town and the minute they turned up they began lining themselves up in formations and banging away on dustbin lids with their baseball bats, beckoning us to attack.

I said to Biffo, "Are these guys for real or what? Because they're behaving like the Zulus in that film with Michael Caine and Stanley Baxter."

He shrugged.

"Dunno, Harry," he said, eyeing them nervously. "But whether they are or not, one thing's certain. They've been watching too much television because that is exactly what the Zulus did in the film of the same name."

"What, the one starring Stanley Baxter and Michael Caine?" I said.

He nodded.

"Well, look what happened to them," I said with a grin on my face. "They were forced to retreat with their tails between their legs despite superior numbers."

He smiled and glanced anxiously at the Birmingham hordes who were still banging away on their dustbins before turning back to me.

"Well, let's hope your battleplan works," he said worriedly, "because if it doesn't we'll be in serious trouble here. Just look at their numbers. We're outnumbered four to one."

"It's not my plan," I replied. "It's Dani Lia's."

"Dani Lia's," he said, with more than a hint of trepidation in his voice, such was the fear the name Dani Lia invoked. "Christ, I've heard of him. Isn't he the guy who confronted Portsmouth's firm with a shotgun in his hand, before forcing them into a barn and setting light to it?"

"That's him," I said with admiration in my voice.

"And knocked out Bournemouth's top boy with one punch, despite the latter being one of the hardest men in the country?"

"That's him," I replied again.

"Christ," said Biffo. "When did you meet him?"

"I didn't," I said, with a widening grin. "I just rang the pub the Wigan firm hangs out in, saying I wanted his advice on how to beat the Birmingham Zulus and eventually one of his firm rang me back detailing the plan that I outlined in the pub to you and the rest of the DLF earlier."

"So you didn't meet or speak to him directly," Biffo replied. "Well, I can't say I'm surprised. I hear the man is a ghost. Not even his firm know much about him."

"He's not a ghost," I replied, "he's a legend and I mean a fucking legend."

Biffo smiled.

"He must be if you think so, Harry."

He paused and shifted awkwardly on his feet.

"Still, do you think this plan of his will work? It sounds weird to me."

It sounded weird to me too and if anybody but Dani Lia had thought of it, I would have put it down to the ramblings of a madman. But as I said earlier, the man was a genius. He would come up with all sort of ingenious ways to stop a rival firm coming onto his patch and taking liberties, from posing as British rail officials and putting them on the wrong train so they wouldn't get to Wigan and run amok on his turf, to getting girls in short skirts to ply them with booze laced with sedatives before dumping them in fields in the middle of nowhere, leaving them to wonder what the fuck was going on when they woke up and found themselves staring into the faces of a herd of cows.

The plan he had come up with to stop Birmingham's firm was weird even by his standards and I mean weird. What it entailed was asking the Birmingham firm to meet us on some wasteland away from preying eyes and do battle there.

That was not unusual because rival firms often agreed to meet at out of the way locations and away from the preying eyes of the police and other busy bodies. That way you could have a good ruck with one of your rivals without having to worry about the old bill stepping in and spoiling the show.

What was unusual however, was that Dani told us to turn up an hour before the ruck was to take place and then dig a large hole about 50 metres wide before covering it with cloth and throwing soil over it to hide the fact there was a large hole there.

Bizarre it may sound but football hooligans always stand facing each other before doing battle in a pre-arranged ruck, just like opposing armies always used to do in the good old days. It was as though they were waiting for everybody to signify they were ready before things kicked off.

So Dani's plan was quite simple. Stand on one side of the hole, goad Birmingham's firm into rushing forward and attacking you and then stand back and watch as these goons go tumbling into the hole.

Well, the plan worked as all Dani's plans did and Birmingham's firm found themselves at the bottom of a large hole, looking somewhat bog-eyed and scratching their heads in bewilderment.

It was so funny that neither I nor the rest of the DLF could stop laughing and we drove back to our local boozer in a state of hysterics.

We had already decided by then that we weren't going to put Dani's next stage of his battleplan into action because it was so crazy that even I shirked from it.

What he had suggested we do was to wait until the Zulus had fallen down the hole before pouring tarmac over them and burying them down there for all eternity.

MICHAEL PARKINSON

At the start of December 1978, I was at the pinnacle of my career as a hooligan. In fact, not only was I recognised as the hardest and most feared hooligan in the country, but my fame was spreading far and wide beyond the violent confines of the hooligan world. I blame the *Hooligan News* for that.

I hadn't realised it at the time but when they posted pictures of me in their newspaper it wasn't just football hooligans who had read it with interest. It seemed somebody from the BBC had done so too and thought it would make a great story and the next thing I know, I'm being asked to appear on Michael Parkinson's chat show.

I couldn't believe it when I got the phone call and with good reason. Back in the 70,s *Parkinson* wasn't just a talk show. It was the ultimate talk show. It was said that you weren't anybody in Hollywood or back here in the UK unless you had been on *Parkinson*. For this reason, there was always an endless streak of celebrities and politicians doing their utmost to worm a place on the show, especially as over fourteen million people tuned in every Saturday to watch it.

Indeed, over the last year, Muhammed Ali, Clint Eastwood, Shirley Bassey, Margaret Thatcher, Telly Savalas and Ryan O'Neal had been interviewed on *Parkinson* so that should give you some idea of the calibre of the people involved.

I was very sceptical when I got the phone call asking me to go on, and I kept saying to Monica and everybody else down at the pub, "It must be a joke, it must be a joke," but eventually it became clear it wasn't any such thing, and after Monica and everybody else I knew had advised me to go on I agreed to do so and a date was set for me to appear on the show on 7 January 1978.

But right from the start the whole thing was surreal. I was told a huge black limousine would roll up on the estate at around one o'clock in the afternoon to whisk me to London and sure enough it did.

I don't remember much about the trip because the limo was so damn comfortable that I nodded off and when I woke up we were pulling into BBC headquarters.

The chauffeur opened the door and when I got out of the car this middle-aged woman in a suit stepped forward with her hand outstretched.

"Mr Hatchet, very nice to meet you. I'm Miss Moran. One of Mr Parkinson's assistants. Oh!"

She glanced at my blue jeans, white top, green jacket and Dr Marten boots and looked as though she was going to have an apoplexy.

"Oh, Mr Hatchet," she said with a look of alarm on her face, "you're not going to go on *Parkinson* looking like that. Surely."

I stared at her.

"Looking like what?" I replied. "What the fuck's wrong with me?"

She didn't answer that. Instead, she just said, "Follow me" and I was led into the building and what a building it was. Talk about Wendy's Parlour looking like a rabbit warren! This place did too, only on a much grander scale.

I was led down one corridor and then another and all the time I was thinking my god, the money they spend here must be phenomenal. I mean, it was like a space station, it really was, with telephone sets and computers everywhere. Even the furniture was the very best and I said to her, "My god, there must be some money here and if this was Derby, somebody would be breaking in every week to rob the joint," and she just gave me another funny look before throwing open a door and saying, "Wait in there."

Inside the place was like a palace, and as soon as the woman closed the door behind her, leaving me to my own devices, a bar tender appeared out of nowhere and asked if he could get me anything.

"A beer would be nice," I replied.

"Certainly, sir," he said. "Would you care for anything to eat?"

For some reason the question surprised me not that I was complaining. I was famished.

"Sure," I said. "Do you have a menu?"

He handed me one, and what a menu it was. Talk about fine dining, you wouldn't believe the things that were on it. Duck, lobster, steak, caviar, gateau, things in French I could not pronounce but which the man assured me were oysters and other gastric delights.

I'm a plain sort of guy so I plumped for a ham omelette and fries and he vanished behind the small bar in the corner, leaving me to my own devices.

So I plonked myself down in an armchair and laid back and it was so comfortable that just like in the limo, I dozed off and it was a good twenty minutes before I was woken by the bartender, waiter, or whatever he was and informed me my dinner was ready.

He wasn't kidding. He pointed to a table and as I strolled over, there was my omelette and fries next to a large pint of stout beer.

I said to him, "How much do I owe you, mate?" and he said, "Nothing, sir. As a guest of the corporation everything is free."

So I tucked into my grub and by god it was delicious. In fact, it was that good it wouldn't have surprised me if it had been cooked by Fanny Craddock.

Then the door open and in walked this smart-looking woman wearing a suit and top.

"Another beer, please," I said to her.

She looked at me blankly and said, "I beg your pardon, young man?"

"Another beer," I snapped, "and be quick about it. I'm due on *Parkinson* soon."

"You're due on *Parkinson*?" she said, surprised.

"Certainly am," I said, pointing a forkful of omelette at her. "But who the fuck are you? I thought you were the waitress."

She began choking and for a minute or two had difficulty finding her breath and then when she did, she glared down at me with bulging eyes.

"Who the fuck am I?" she repeated incredulously. "Young man, I'm one of the actresses in crossroads."

"Crossroads," I replied, scooping some more omelette on my fork. "You mean that poxy show set in a Birmingham motel?"

She nodded.

"With that halfwit Benny in it?"

Again, she nodded.

"Think it's a load of crap," I replied. "Watched it once and that was enough because—"

Just then the door opened, and my eyes nearly popped out of my head. I knew there were other guests appearing on the show with me but I didn't know who they were because two of them had to pull out at the last moment and they were looking for replacements, but I never in my wildest dreams expected one of them to be Roger Moore. I mean for God's sake, this guy played James Bond and I had watched him many times at the cinema and on TV.

The woman too, was clearly taken aback and it was a good few seconds before she was able to compose herself and find her voice, not that the man seemed to notice. He just walked towards her with his hand outstretched and said to her in a beautifully polished accent, "How do you do, I'm Roger Moore."

Well, she buckled under his gaze, and shook his hand, and then the great man turned to me.

"Hello there," he said, beaming kindly. "I'm Roger Moore."

I put my knife and fork down.

"How you doing, mate?" I cried, shaking his hand warmly. "I've seen you on television many times. I'm a great James Bond fan."

He smiled even more and then the door opened again, and in walked Michael Parkinson. The man made a beeline for Roger Moore, perhaps in recognition that out of all of us, he was by far the most famous and therefore, in Parkinson's eyes at least, the most important.

"Hi, Roger," he said beaming from side to side. "It's nice to see you again. How's life with you?"

They exchanged pleasantries, and then Parkinson turned to the woman, which suggested to me that he considered her more important than me in the pecking order, though God knows why, I mean, she was just some poxy little actress in a poxy little soap, but there you go.

He engaged in polite conversation with her before turning to me and extending his hand.

"And you must be Harry Hatchett."

"I am mate, yes," I said as we shook hands. "Pleased to meet you."

We exchanged small talk and then he quickly got down to business and explained what would happen next.

I won't go into the ins and outs because that will take forever, but it ended up with me being sent to a makeup room, where the makeup artists sat me in front of a chair and rubbed some cream on my face and tried to pamper me up.

It was a bit of a farce really, I mean, being a skinhead I didn't have any hair to comb back and with me having such a handsome mush, what could they do to me that would make me more beautiful than I was?

Then I was escorted down a corridor and told I was due on set in two minutes' time.

INTERVIEWED

I don't know if any of you have ever been interviewed live on TV but trust me, it's quite a daunting experience, or at least it was for me.

I was behind stage when the programme went on air, and I heard somebody say, "Three, two, one," before the voice cut out and Parkinson's voice sailed through the air.

"My guests today include Brenda Bingham, star of *Crossroads* and a familiar face on our television sets."

The audience went wild.

"Hollywood legend and James Bond himself, Roger Moore."

The audience went even more wild.

"But first, a man whose name may not be familiar to you all, but in the world of football hooliganism has certainly made a name for himself. Firstly, by smashing hell out of any firm that dared invade his manor and put many if not all of its members in hospital, and secondly by taking on hooligan's top boys which had them cowering behind doors shaking with fear. Ladies and gentlemen, a round of applause for Mr Harry Hatchett."

Music blared through the air, an assistant told me to walk through the door, and that was it. I found myself on set, walking up to Parkinson who had his hand outstretched, and fourteen million viewers up and down the country watching me.

"Good to meet you, Harry," he said, shaking my hand warmly.

"How you doing, mate?" I replied cordially.

He guided me to a seat. I sat down, he took a seat opposite me, the audience stopped clapping, and the interview began.

"Now, Mr Hatchet," he said in his gruff Yorkshire accent, "or Harry if I may call you that, I described you in my introduction as a legend in the world of football hooliganism but for those of my viewers who don't know you, and I suspect that will be most, will be wondering why."

"Well, it's quite simple," I said, "I'm a legend because I'm the hardest hooligan in the country. I've fought the best and I've beat the best."

"Oh really," said Parkinson, casting a gleeful glance at the audience. "How did you do that?"

"By kicking fuck out of them," I said, glancing at him with an incredulous stare. "How the fuck do you think I did it?"

Parkinson coughed, and I leaned forward in my seat. "Well, either that or I did it by smashing my hatchets down on their worthless little skulls, and leaving them needing hospital treatment for a week, perhaps longer."

"Hatchets," said Parkinson, in apparent surprise. "Oh yes, amongst hooligans you're known as Hatchet Harry aren't you, in recognition of your tendency for attacking rival fans with hatchets."

He turned to the audience as he said that and there were gasps of horror.

"Well yes, I am, actually. But I don't know what that lot over there are looking so shocked about," I replied, pointing at the audience.

"It's only natural to smash a hatchet over the skull of rival firms if they are taking liberties, surely."

He asked me what a rival firm was before I told him they were fellow hooligans who followed one club or another, and who every match day did battle with whatever firm their team was playing on the day, before he expressed surprise that such things were going on and asked how I had become involved in football hooliganism in the first place.

"By accident, mate," I replied. "That's how. I was coming back from a National Front march when the coach I was on was attacked by the reds, so after I kicked fuck out of them I got talking to Biffo, a fellow NF supporter who told me he was impressed by my fighting skills and that he was a member of the Derby Fairy Cakes."

Parkinson blinked. "The who?" he said, casting an amused glance at the audience.

"The Derby Fairy Cakes," I replied. "It's what the Derby hooligans called themselves before I took over the firm."

The audience burst out laughing when I said that, particularly as Parkinson was looking at them with a comical expression on his face, before urging me to explain so I did.

I told him that the reason the Derby firm called themselves the Fairy Cakes was because there was a huge factory in the town which made fairy cakes and the people who were running the firm at the time thought it would be a good idea to call themselves after it.

I said all firms had names such as the Chelsea Headhunters, Millwall's F-Troop, and West Ham's Inter City firm but as soon as I took over at Derby, things soon changed and I renamed the firm the Derby Lunatic Fringe. A name I told him which now strikes fear into firms int the country.

Thoughout this Parkinson was looking at me as though he couldn't quite believe his ears, and even the audience were looking aghast, but then what happened next nearly had Parkinson falling out of his chair.

"Want to see my hatchets?" I asked him with a slight grin.

"You've got them here?" he said with a look of pure astonishment on his face.

"Course I have, mate," I said. "I carry them everywhere with me."

I pulled them out of my jacket and stood in front of him, clutching one in each hand.

The man's reaction was quite comical. His eyes had nearly popped out of his head and his complexion went as white as snow.

"These … these are the hatchets you used to attack your rivals," he said, barely able to get the words out.

"Of course they are, mate," I replied, as I handed them to him. "What the fuck do you think they are, souvenirs?"

There was a slight ripple of laughter from the audience as I said that, which surprised me because up to then they had been looking just as shocked as my host but he wasn't finished yet.

"Are … are these real?" he said, looking at me as though I was some kind of deranged lunatic.

"Of course they're not, mate. If they were, then half the hooligans in the country would be lying in a graveyard with their heads chopped off now, wouldn't they. No, they're imitations but very good ones. They're made of rubber. Feel."

He did, and then muttered, "I see" before blurting out that imitations or not they were still very dangerous weapons which could cause somebody great injury. "Don't you think, Harry?" he added.

"Of course I do," I replied, shocked that he needed to ask. "What the fuck do you think I carry them round with me for? And why do you think any firm who crosses my path tend to wind up in extensive care?"

Again the audience burst out into laughter and Parkinson once more looked as though he couldn't believe his ears, but time was up. All guests were interviewed for a quarter of an hour and the minutes had certainly flown by. But I could tell there was one thing more he wanted to know and I was right.

"Tell me, Harry," he said, glancing towards the audience for moral support. "I'm only asking this because the audience and viewers around the country will want to know but is it only football hooligans you have attacked with your hatchets, or have you attacked anybody else?"

"Well, like who, for example?" I said, puzzled.

"Like women and children for instance."

"Never, mate, why do you ask?"

"Well, if you don't mind me saying so, you do strike me as a man who has an insatiable blood lust."

"A blood lust," I said, puzzled. "You mean like a vampire?"

He laughed. "If you like."

I stared at him.

"What the fuck do you take me for, mate?" I retorted angrily." Some kind of weirdo?"

Parkinson turned to the audience and smiled, the latter laughed, and that was it. The interview was over.

Then it was the turn of that stupid bitch from *Crossroads* and she came out all smiling and waving and looking as though butter wouldn't melt in her mouth, before shaking Parkinson's hand and then mine, and then sitting down in her chair and waiting for the interview to begin.

To be perfectly honest, I wasn't sure why I was still there because I had been interviewed and now the spotlight had moved on, but I was later told that all guests remained on set even after they had been interviewed because that was how they did things on Parkinson.

I won't bore you with what that stupid bitch had to say. To do so would only send you to sleep as I'm sure it did the audience and the millions of viewers watching.

It simply involved making out she was a poor girl who had got lucky when the producer of *Crossroads* saw her performing on stage and asked her to audition for a part in the show. Or to put it another way, she shagged him and got the role.

Then Roger Moore made his appearance. No sooner had he walked onto the stage than the audience went wild and everybody was on their feet. I've never seen anything like it. My God did that man have presence. Anyway, he came up and shook hands with Parkinson and the rest of us and we all took our seats.

I won't go into the ins and outs of what was said because although it was interesting, it would take too long and anyway, you can see it for yourself by logging on to YouTube and typing in 'Roger Moore, Parkinson 1978', and seeing for yourself.

But the best bit is what happened afterwards. As he did on every occasion Parkinson would then have an open discussion with all three guests by asking them a question about themselves and then turning to the other two and enquiring from them what they thought about the issue they had raised.

Well, on this occasion he asked Roger Moore about famous James Bond villains and whether he thought I would make a good villain, given I was proficient with my hatchets and had a trademark tool, just like Odd Job in *Goldfinger* with his deadly hat. He turned to Brenda Bingham and said to her with a smile on his face, "So, what do you think. Brenda? Would Hatchet Harry here make a good Bond villain, do you think?"

The audience laughed, and Bingham turned to them with a grin before saying in a somewhat sarcastic tone, "Well, the man's clearly a thug so yes I do. What's more, he's also a freak of the weirdest kind. I mean really. Look at him with his Dr Marten boots, white top, and braces. The man should be in a circus."

The audience burst out laughing and I turned to her angrily.

"And where should you be?" I snapped. "No, don't tell me, I'll tell you. You should be in a fucking brothel, that's where you should be. I mean, look at you with your fancy suit, high heeled shoes and lipstick. You're nothing but am ambitious little tart who is prepared to use sex to get what you want, aren't you."

The colour drained from her face, but I wasn't finished yet.

"What's more," I cried, waving an angry finger at her, "that little story you told us before, the one where the producer took a shine to you, and asked you to audition for a part in *Crossroads*, which is how you ended up in the show, it's a load of crap. Do you really want to know how she got the part in *Crossroads*?" I said, turning to the audience.

"Yes," they shouted, fascinated.

"She shagged him," I said. "That's what happened. The producer fancied her, so she shagged him and got the part that way."

The audience gasped, Moore and Parkinson looked at me in disbelief, while the woman herself went ballistic and leapt from her seat.

"How fucking dare you," she yelled. "How fucking dare you."

"Shut it, you little tart," I cried. "And stop playing to the camera."

She snatched the hatchets from my pockets.

"Give me them back now," I yelled, jumping from my seat angrily.

"Why?" she said. "Are you going to hit me with them like you do everybody else?"

I opened my mouth to speak but she slapped me around the face and yelled, "Well go on, big boy, hit me with them. Hit me."

I didn't need telling twice.

I smashed the hatchet down so hard on her skull that she slumped to the ground and rolled down the steps before coming to a standstill at the bottom and lying there in a pool of blood.

The show ended with millions of viewers watching horrified as I stood there with my hatchets in my hand and lips curled up in a grin, and the theme music to *Parkinson* blaring out in the background, which it always did once the show was over.

ARRESTED

As soon as the show was over, I was bundled into a car and driven back to Derby at top speed. You would've thought I'd been arrested and charged with assault wouldn't you, but I think the producers were in a state of shock and just wanted me out of the way as quickly as possible, so I was driven home and that was that. I wasn't their problem anymore.

The next day the papers were full of the story.

Hatchet man runs amok on Parkinson, said the *Daily Record*.

Lunatic knocks out Crossroads *actress,* ran the headline in *The Sun*.

Famous actress gets it, from the *Daily Mirror*.

Actress gets clobbered, screamed the front page of the *Daily Express*.

Hatchet man steals the show, ran the cover of the *Guardian*.

It was amazing stuff and my parents were really proud of me when I came down the stairs the next day and showed me the papers.

But the best bit was when I switched on the television and found myself plastered all over the TV channels. Indeed, the *News at One* was full of the story and kept playing the bit when I whacked the woman over the head with my hatchet over and over again. But that wasn't all.

It's a funny thing but when your face is plastered all over the news, the world and his wife know who you are and stare at you like you are an exhibit in the zoo. I couldn't walk down the street without people stopping me and telling me how much they enjoyed watching me giving the bitch her just desserts.

It was the same in the pub. The minute I walked in there was an almighty cheer and everybody was eager to buy me a pint, but it was Tommo who had that honour. It had become his custom to buy me drinks and because he relished that honour I saw no reason to upset him by denying him that privilege now and within minutes, I was part of a merry band swigging beer and discussing my new found fame.

Then things got really bizarre. By the following morning it wasn't just the BBC and other UK news channels reporting the story and showing footage of me whacking that stupid bitch over the head with my hatchet, but news stations in France, Germany, Australia, Canada and America, to name but a few.

The first I knew about it, however, was when my mum came running into my bedroom the next morning to inform me the house was being besieged by reporters.

I leapt from my bed and grabbed my hatchets. If there is one thing I hate more than anything it is being woken from my beauty sleep.

"Don't worry, Mum," I said, as I bounded down the stairs. "I'll soon disperse them."

I threw open the door and leapt outside.

"Right, you little bastards," I yelled, "where are you? I'll teach you to wake me from my beauty sleep."

Then I got the shock of my life.

When Mum said besieged by reporters, I thought she meant one or two older guys in shabby macs with wrinkled faces and cigarettes dangling out the side of their mouths. Instead I got flashing lights and hordes of men and women in smart suits holding microphones and pointing them at me while guys with TV cameras stood behind them.

"Morning, Harry!" one said, with a smile on his face.

"Just woken up have you, Harry?" said a brown-haired man with a grin.

"Were you hoping to kill Brenda Bingham when you smashed a hatchet over her head?" asked a weedy-looking man in a blue coat.

"Nice birthday suit, Harry," said a red-haired woman with a twinkle in her eye.

I stared at her. I had been so keen to get outside and smash a hatchet over the heads of those who had woken me from my beauty sleep, I had not bothered to put any clothes on and as such, I was now standing there with nothing but my boxer shorts on and a hatchet in each hand, and people all over the world watching it live on TV with a mixture of astonishment and amusement on their faces.

Even my mum and dad were smiling, and I was just about to retreat hastily, when there was the sound of police sirens wailing through the air and cars coming to a screeching halt, and before I knew it police officers had wrestled me to the ground and were reading me my rights.

"Harry Hatchet," cried one. "You're under arrest for assault. You don't have to say anything but anything you do say may be taken down and used in evidence against you."

With that I was thrown unceremoniously in the back of a police van, before being driven away at top speed, leaving my parents and hordes of journalists gaping after me in bewilderment.

Down at the station I was hurled before the front desk and mocked by the sergeant on duty.

"Gentlemen," he said, turning to his colleagues with a big grin on his face. "You should feel honoured because we have a real celebrity here. In fact we have none other than the infamous Hatchet Harry. A man so hard, he feels the need to whack women over their heads with his rubber hatchets. Is that not so, Harry?"

"Too fucking right," I said.

He picked up the hatchets in question that an officer had placed thoughtfully before him and studied them with interest.

"And what do we have here?" he said, weighing them in his hand. "Why it's the hatchets themselves, including the one he whacked that poor woman with." He paused and said with a big grin, "Which one did you whack her with, Harry?"

"Don't answer that, Mr Hatchet," cried a voice from behind.

I wheeled around.

A smartly dressed man carrying a briefcase and wearing a bowler hat stood there, with two women just as well clad behind him.

"Who the fuck are you?" cried the sergeant, glaring at him angrily.

The man walked up to the desk and fixed the sergeant with a defiant gaze and the latter quickly modified his tone.

"I mean, eh. Can I help you, sir?"

The man calmly placed his briefcase on the desk and adjusted his pince nez which only added to the feeling that it was he and not the police who were now running the show.

"Certainly," he said, handing him a card, "you can tell me what my client has been arrested for."

The sergeant glanced at the card and then back at him.

"Assault, sir," he replied briskly. "Mr Hatchet has been arrested on suspicion of assaulting a well-known personality on television the day before yesterday. On *Parkinson* to be precise."

"Ah yes," said the smartly dressed man, with a slight frown, "I saw the show myself, but I must say I'm somewhat confused that it is my client you have arrested on suspicion of assault."

"Oh yes?" said the sergeant nervously.

"But yes," the man replied, with a raised eyebrow. "I mean, if my memory serves me right, the lady in question grabbed my client's hatchets and when he reasonably and justifiably asked for them back, she slapped him across the face."

He paused and fixed the sergeant with an incredulous stare.

"And you say it is my client who has been arrested on suspicion of assault. But surely, it's the other way around? Surely, it is the woman who should be charged with attacking my client. Or does the law allow celebrities to strike ordinary members of the public with immunity?"

Once again, he fixed the sergeant with a mild enquiring glare and once again the latter buckled under his gaze.

"Still," he replied, grabbing his briefcase, "before you interview him I would like to confer with my client in private. I take it you have a room which is free."

A minute later I found myself in a room with the well-dressed man, but I didn't need to ask who he was.

My father had told me about Gerald Bickerstaffe, but this was the first time I had ever met him, which, given he lived just outside Derby and was a legend in NF circles, was quite surprising.

He was an Oxford-educated barrister who had made a fortune defending fellow patriots when the establishment charged them with one crime or another. In the 1950s for example, he had successfully defended Oswald Mosley on a charge of libel and in the sixties had successfully defended John Tyndall on a charge of assault.

I shouldn't have been as surprised as I was when he told me that my parents had asked him to come down to the station and represent me but I was, because he was one of the best paid barristers in the land, and cost a fortune to hire so I couldn't understand how my parents could afford him, even with the money my mother was raking in from the brothel – eh, massage parlour, so I asked him and he just smiled and said, "Don't worry about that, Harry, the authorities will take care of that. I assure you."

A few minutes later the sergeant informed us that the police had had a change of heart and would not be charging me with assault.

I had to laugh at that.

Mr Bickerstaffe had put his arguments so elegantly and with such potency that it was difficult to see what else they could do.

What happened next virtually took my breath away.

No sooner had we stepped outside the station than hordes of reporters came rushing up waving their microphones in my faces or flashing their cameras as they had done earlier.

I was gobsmacked and said to my lawyer, "What the fuck's going on? I hadn't expected them to be here, are they following me about or what?"

"Of course they are, Harry," he said with a slight grin, "what did you expect?"

He then turned to the throng of reporters and said in a raised voice, "If you don't mind, ladies and gentlemen, I have a statement to make."

I won't go into the details of what he said but he began by expressing incredulity that I had been arrested for assault, given that I was the one who had been assaulted, before going on to say that he fully expected the police to arrest Miss Brenda Bingham for it, and he would expect them to call Roger Moore as the chief witness at any subsequent trial.

I'm not sure who looked the more astounded, me or the journalists milling round.

ARSENAL

The next day I made national headlines again.

Hatchet Harry arrested for assault ran the headline in one newspaper.

Harry claims Crossroads *star assaulted him* said another.

James Bond star to be called as chief witness said a third.

I couldn't believe it and had to pinch myself just to make sure I wasn't dreaming.

People at the pub couldn't believe it either, especially when television crews began turning up and asking them what it was like having a well-known celebrity in their midst.

I had to laugh at that because I had never been described as a celebrity before, but I wasn't complaining. I was known as the hardest hooligan in the country, so a celebrity is precisely what I was.

Celebrity or not I was a hooligan first and foremost, and by the beginning of 1979 I was back to doing what I do best and showing hooligans all around the country who really was the top boy. That wasn't hard because we came up against the pathetic likes of Bolton Wanderers Cuckoo Boys, West Bromwich Albion Section Five and Queen's Park Rangers Bush Babies who quite frankly couldn't punch a hole through a paper bag, but at least they didn't brick it and hide behind closed doors like the Chelsea Headhunters or Middlesbrough's Frontline, though they probably wished they had after I smashed my hatchets down on their miserable skulls and treated them to a free stay in hospital, courtesy of the Derby Lunatic Fringe.

Then we came up against the Arsenal Gooners and this was another of those firms who were allowing niggers into their ranks which made them a real target in my eyes but worse, far worse, their top boy was a nigger named Bear and I was particularly keen to meet him because he had been harassing NF members outside Highbury and stopping them going about their lawful business, which included handing out leaflets and trying to recruit new members to the party.

I mean, who was he to tell the NF where they could and couldn't leaflet or recruit new members? It was a liberty, that's what it was, a diabolical liberty and I was dying to make him pay for it.

Come the day, however, we didn't bother to go looking for them because we were playing Arsenal on our home patch so I thought we'd let the bastards find us. Our pub was just across the road from the baseball ground, so it shouldn't have been too difficult for them to locate our whereabouts, particularly as I sent word to them on the grapevine where we were.

But then a totally unexpected thing happened, these goons attacked the pub just as a BBC camera crew was driving past on the way to film the match and they quickly stopped the van and jumped out and began filming everything.

In fact, their timing was so good because they had barely switched their cameras on when the pub doors swung open and out I came, hatchets in hand and laying into any Arsenal thug in my way, particularly a red-haired youth with a spotty face and long pointed nose who came hurtling towards me with a knife in his hand, only to have a hatchet smashed into his face and he hit the deck quicker than a greyhound out of a trap.

His mate with a tattoo on his face and hair curled back in a pony tail soon joined him, as did two huge skinheads with a hammer in their hands, a fat bloke in his thirties and a brown-haired numbskull who screamed the place down as my hatchet buried itself in his head.

I was loving every minute of it and with the rest of the DLF laying into them, it was clear we were getting the upper hand, but until I did battle with the Bear I could not consider it a good day.

The problem was though, I couldn't see the bastard because as soon as I put one Gooner down, another one came at me. So I continued to kick, whack and knock out anybody who got in my way, which at times was farcical because as soon as the Arsenal firm saw me coming at them with hatchets in hand, they would cry, "Fuck me, it's him, it's Hatchet Harry" before they felt the full weight of my hatchets on their skulls and fell to the ground too.

Then I caught sight of the Bear at last. The bastard came flying out of an alleyway with three skinheads behind him and I learned later that he had left a couple of our lads out cold and in need of intensive care. I couldn't care less about them and in fact, if he hadn't put them in intensive care I would probably have done so myself. These idiots had let a nigger get the better of them so a month in hospital feeding off a drip was the best place for them.

Then the Bear caught sight of me and his eyes nearly popped out of his head. "Fuck me," he yelled, "there's the bastard now. That's Hatchet Harry."

As quick as a flash he was storming towards me with the skinheads in tow and I clutched my hatchets tighter and braced myself for the impending encounter.

Before he could get to me, Biffo and a bunch of other lads began streaming into him and fists and boots were flying everywhere.

I gave him his due, the Bear was putting up stiff resistance and with those great big hands of his, he knocked out a few of our lads but by now we had the superior numbers and as most of their firm were either lying unconscious or taking a pounding, it was clear all I needed to do was to stand back and let Biffo and the rest of the lads take care of the Bear themselves.

I could not just stand there and let them have all the fun though. I had to step in and give the black bastard a good seeing to myself. I mean after all, he had come to do me harm and so he should expect nothing less.

So I pushed the rest of my firm out the way so I could have him all to myself and then got to work. I say got to work but there wasn't much I could do because he was all bloodied and dazed and barely conscious.

Barely conscious wasn't good enough for me. I wanted the bastard out for the count and sampling hospital food within the hour. So I grabbed him by the head and brought the full weight of my hatchet down on him.

"That's for all those NF paper sellers you have been harassing outside your ground," I cried, as he slumped to the ground with blood pouring out of him, clearly in need of the medical services.

FAME

That wasn't the end of the matter. I had been so busy knocking hell out of the Bear and his firm that I had forgotten that the BBC were filming it all and by tea time the whole country knew about it because it was plastered all over the news.

I was ecstatic and the mood inside the pub when I entered the following day was jubilant.

"Well done, Harry," cried one worthy.

"You're the man, Harry," cried another.

"We love you, Harry," said Tommo, handing me a beer.

"Harry for Prime Minister," yelled a youth with a drunken leer on his face.

Even Monica who rarely showed any emotion at all couldn't quite believe it and raised her glass in mock salute. "I have to hand it to you, Harry," she said with a widening grin. "You may be a bit of a rogue, but at least you're a famous one."

"Famous," I said, as we touched glasses, "I'm not just famous. I'm infamous."

The next day I was in the public eye again because it turned out that the BBC hadn't just been filming the altercation outside the pub, but had taken pictures of it, and so there I was on the front page of the *Sun*, *Daily Mail* and other national dailies smashing my hatchet down on the nigger's skull as his goons lay out cold around him. Not that the newspapers were worried about that.

Hatchet Harry saves the day, cried the headline in the *Daily Mail*.

Harry the hero of the hour, said the *Sun*.

Harry comes to pub rescue, shouted out the *Daily Express*.

It was absolutely brilliant, my favourite headline was the one which appeared in the *Daily Tattler,* under the heading, *Harry goes bear hunting* and underneath was a picture of me smashing a hatchet down on the Bear's head with my lips curled back in a grin and the nigger himself looking as though his eyes were popping out of his head.

These days no paper in the land would publish a picture of a nigger getting done over by a far-right thug, let alone gloat over it on the front cover of their rag but back then things were different and because of it my fame started to grow and grow and grow.

Then things got even more bizarre.

The phone rang and when I picked it up a well-polished voice said, "Harry Hatchet?"

"Yes," I replied.

"Better known as Hatchet Harry?"

"Yes," I replied again.

"I'm Arron Levy, the owner of Levy Sportswear. Perhaps you've heard of us."

I certainly had. Levy Sportswear had shops everywhere and but I was still puzzled as to the purpose of the call so I asked him why he was calling me. To cut a long story short it seemed he had seen all the publicity I had been getting and thought he could make money for us both by plastering my face on football tops with Derby County colours on them.

I thought he was joking, and told him so, but he just said, "Listen, Harry, you may not see it but I do, and to prove it I'm going to send you a contract and if you like what it says, then get back to me. If you don't, then no hard feelings. OK?"

True to his word the contract was delivered and when I read it, I could not believe my eyes because the man was offering me a flat-out payment of two thousand pounds if I signed it and back in 1979, that was enough to buy you a house with change to spare.

Not only that, he was also offering me a royalty of ten per cent on any item he sold with my name and face on it, and when I say my name on it I mean my nickname, Hatchett Harry and I just could not believe anybody would do such a thing – I really couldn't.

I got my lawyer to check out the contract very carefully in case there was any funny business and once he said he was happy with it, I signed and within a month, Derby County shirts bearing my face began to hit the production line.

NF MEETING

So by the summer of 1979 my life was on the up, my fame was spreading far and wide, and shirts bearing my handsome mug were selling everywhere. The money was rolling in thick and fast, and I wasn't doing a damn thing to earn it. Indeed, that was the funny thing about the money I earned from the contract I had with Levy. It was Levy who produced the shirts, sold the shirts, everything. All I had to do was sit back and watch as the royalties poured in and nothing else. Hard life wasn't it.

Then my mother threw a spanner in the works.

"Harry," she said, one morning at breakfast, "I've got a bit of bad news for you."

"What's that?" I said.

"Levy is Jewish."

I stared at her. "Levy is Jewish?"

"Yes," she replied nervously. "Levy is Jewish."

I continued to stare at her angrily. "But why didn't you tell me this before?" I protested.

She shook her head apologetically. "I'm sorry, Harry, I thought you knew, after all Levy is a Jewish name."

Well, she was right about that, it was. In fact, it was one of the most popular Jewish names around. She wasn't finished yet. "We have another problem, Harry, Bernie Harper's not happy about the fact you are working with a Jew. He says, if you don't cancel the deal with Levy he'll have you drummed out of the NF at the next NF meeting."

"He does, does he," I replied. "Well, when's the next NF meeting?"

"Tonight," she replied.

"Leave it with me," I said.

Come six o' clock, I drove over to a huge farm on the edge of town where the meeting was to be held, along with Biffo and the lads and pulled up outside a large black barn. My parents were with me and as I walked in the atmosphere inside changed considerably. Whereas before there had been hordes of skinheads, toffs, and elderly men talking in groups, now they stopped and gazed at me in trepidation.

Bernie Harper was there and even though I had never met him before, or even knew him by sight, I recognised him immediately. My parents had told me all about him so I knew he was a fifty something goon who had left the Conservative Party and joined the NF in the hope of rising up the ranks and becoming a big fish in a small pond rather than a small fish in a big pond so to speak.

Indeed, he had recently been making moves to have my dad stripped as NF organiser, so he could be made organiser himself, and the reason I recognised him was because he always wore a tweed suit and never went anywhere unless his nephew, a seven foot gorilla called Sidney Harper, was with him like he was now. Thanks to my media profile he recognised me too.

That said, despite the fact he had called a meeting to have me thrown out of the party on the charge of race mixing with Jews, he greeted me like an old friend.

"Harry," he said, with his hand outstretched. "I'm very pleased to meet you. I've heard so much about you. How are you doing?"

"Not too bad, mate," I replied, shaking his hand warmly much to everybody's surprise.

"Now then, Harry," he said, guiding me to a table which had been laid out in the warmest part of the barn. "Would you care for a drink before we begin? How about a nice glass of orange juice?"

"Delighted, old boy," I said, putting on the old plum.

He guided me to a table which contained jugs of orange juice and poured me a glass.

"There you are," he said, handing it to me. "Now how about a bite to eat before we start the meeting?"

"Lovely," I said, before grabbing a plate and tucking into the spread that had been laid out and what a spread it was. Sandwiches, pies, crisps, chicken legs, assorted rice dishes, trifle, cakes, biscuits.

"Oh Harry," he said, once I had piled my plate with lots of the tasty savouries, "would you mind if I started the meeting while you eat, and then afterwards you can have your say?"

"By all means," I said, walking back to the table and putting my plate down.

True to his word, he had his say.

I won't go into the ins and outs of everything he said, because it would take too long, but the gist of his argument was that as I had signed a contract with a Jew, I should be expelled from the NF or at the very least be forced to give the money I had earned to the party.

I don't know what weed this guy had been smoking but whatever it was it must have been good stuff because if he thought I was going to give my money to the party, he was out of his head. I didn't say anything. Instead, I just got up, refilled my glass and resumed my seat and continued to devour my food.

Eventually, he brought his speech to an end and asked if I had anything to say in my defence.

It was at this moment I took my hatchets out of my pocket and smashed them over his miserable head, putting him in hospital for a month.

PORT VALE

After that Mum never brought up the subject of Levy being Jewish again and I never let the fact interfere with our business arrangement. After all, the man was making me so much money I would have been foolish to do so. So I just sat back and let the money pour in and got on with pursuing my career as a hooligan.

That, however, was easily said than done. Fame has its benefits but also its drawbacks as I discovered when Derby were playing Port Vale away. I was really looking forward to knocking hell out of Vale's firm, the Vale Lunatic Fringe (VLF) but the minute I opened my front door I was greeted by hordes of reporters flashing their cameras and shoving microphones in my face.

"Harry, are you looking forward to smashing hell out of Port Vale's hooligan firm?" cried one.

"Got your trusted hatchets with you today, Harry?" cried another.

"How many of the opposition do you think you will put in hospital today, Harry?" cried a third.

It was quite ridiculous, and I had difficulty getting to my front gate, let alone to the match. Still, I finally managed to get to the pub and meet up with the DLF but it was a waste of time because as soon as we set off for the game, hordes of journalists followed us everywhere and so we shot back to the pub and spent the whole afternoon getting pissed in there. What else could we do?

DANI LIA

It was around now that Portsmouth's firm, the 6.57 Crew, turned up in Wigan wanting a ruck with the Wigan Goon Squad for events that had taken place a few months earlier when Dani Lia had confronted them with a shotgun and told them if they ever showed their miserable faces in his town again, he would get his flame thrower out and burn them. So when they turned up on wasteland on the edge of town clutching baseball bats and other assorted weapons, he got his flame thrower out and began firing huge bolts of fire at them, sending them fleeing for their lives, never to be seen in Wigan again.

I told you the man was one crazy son of a bitch, didn't I?

BARBARA BINGHAM

I got a phone call from my lawyer and after pleasantries were exchanged he quickly got down to business.

"Harry," he said, with a touch of glee in his voice, "I have good news for you."

"What's that?" I replied.

"Barbara Bingham's been arrested for assault."

"Barbara Bingham's been arrested for assault," I said slowly. "Well, it's about fucking time. But why the delay?"

"Because she's a celebrity," he said with a slight chuckle, "and the police wanted to be doubly sure they had enough evidence to charge her in case it backfires on them and the person in question sues."

"They didn't with me," I retorted.

"That's because you weren't as famous as you are now," he said, laughing.

Well, that was true, I wasn't, but I was still puzzled as to what happened next, so I asked him.

"It's simple, Harry," he replied briskly. "She'll be charged, and will then have to appear in court."

"Court," I said, surprised. "What the fuck for, seeing as she's pleaded guilty. Surely they should just send her to prison and have done with it."

He laughed again and said that wasn't how things were done. He said that once somebody had pleaded guilty they have to go to court to be sentenced, and even then, they may not get a jail sentence.

"No?" I said, even more surprised. "Why not?"

"Well, they may be ordered to do community service, or receive a suspended sentence, which means they wouldn't go to prison unless they commit any further demeanour. If they do, then they will serve a spell inside."

I smiled. "Well, let's hope she does," I said gleefully.

A week later, I was informed by my lawyer that the Crossroads bitch was to appear at court the following week to be charged with assault and I had to be there in case the magistrates needed to grill me on anything.

I said to my lawyer, "What the fuck will they want to grill me on? She's pleading guilty, isn't she?"

"True," he said. "But they may want you to ascertain how you are coping after the attack. What effect it has on you psychologically, and whether any injuries you sustained have healed."

Well, I didn't have any injuries, because the bitch had only slapped me across the face and it would take a lot more than that to injure me, I can assure you. So I said to him. "Injuries, what fucking injuries? I'm the hardest thug in the country. You don't seriously think a jumped-up little tart like that could injure me?"

He laughed. "No, Harry," he said, "it's not what I think but what the magistrates think that counts, and they may want to ask you about it."

So come the day I travelled down to London and when I arrived at the Magistrates Court, I got the shock of my life. There were hordes of Anti Nazi League protestors there waiting to greet me and the minute they clocked me walking up the street with my lawyer and the rest of my legal team behind me, they began yelling and screaming abuse.

"There's the bastard now," yelled one ANL protestor.

"Should hang the Nazi scumbag," cried another.

I turned to my lawyer. "What the fuck's going on?" I cried. "Why are the Anti Nazi League here?"

"No idea, Harry, but keep walking, don't let them rattle you."

Well, that was easier said than done. The ANL had turned out in large numbers and the nearer I got to the courthouse, the more vocal they got. I found out later that the reason they were there is because they knew I was NF so even though I wasn't there to attend an NF protest, they thought they would come and give me a bit of grief anyway. So all the way to the court all you could hear was people chanting, "Nazi Scum of our Streets, Nazi Scum of Our streets."

I was dying to lay into them and plant my hatchets into their miserable heads but my lawyer had advised me against it and as I respected his advice, I did what he said. Besides, there were too many police officers to prevent me having a punch up with them even if I wanted to. At first, I couldn't understand why there were so many police officers about or members of the press for that matter, until my lawyer pointed out that as both myself and Bingham were celebrities, the world and his wife were interested in ascertaining what happened at court today and the man wasn't kidding.

As I got closer I saw the BBC was there, ITV, everybody. Even foreign TV crews were getting in on the act. I saw TV vans from America, France and even Japan. I thought for fuck's, sake why are the nips so interested in this? Then a horde of reporters came running at me, poking their mikes and cameras in my face.

"How's it going, Harry?" cried one.

"Do you hope your attacker goes to prison?" cried another.

"Looking forward to seeing your attacker get her cupperance?" cried a third.

I could barely hear them because all the time they were asking questions the ANL were yelling, "Nazi Scum of our Streets, Nazi Scum of our Streets" behind me.

It was ridiculous, it really was, especially as every time I answered a question from one reporter another one would stick a mike in my face and say, "What's it like being the victim of a violent assault, Harry?" Or, "Have you recovered from your attack, Harry?" Or, "Are you upset you got beat up by a woman, Harry? What with you being the hardest hooligan in the country."

The last had been asked by a slimy little toe rag with a sly grin on his face and I knew why he had put that particular question to me. He had done so because he knew that making out I had been beaten up by a woman was bound to draw an angry response from me, given I was the hardest hooligan in the country, with a reputation to maintain. So I played a blinder. Instead of butting him in the face and wiping that smarmy smile off his face as I was dying to, I just said, "No comment" and walked into the court building, leaving him with egg on his face and chants of "Nazi Scum of our Streets" blaring out in the background.

Inside the building I was still destined to get no peace. It was packed with journalists and ANL supporters and the minute I spotted them I tuned to my lawyer and said, "Oh, for fuck's sake, not here as well. Can't I get a bit of peace?"

"Don't worry, Harry," he said smiling. "They're not allowed to harass you in here. If they do it would be contempt of court."

"Even those ANL wankers over there?"

"Even them," he said, smiling.

I nodded and entered the courtroom but this too was packed to the rafters with journalists and members of the ANL, and the minute the ANL saw me, they began booing and glaring at me with growls on their faces so I smiled and waved up to them as though they were old friends and this just wound them up even more.

Then a door opened and a voice at the front said, "All rise" and everybody did, before three middle aged men walked in and took their place at the bench. Then for a few seconds the poxy looking git in the middle fumbled about with a few papers before glancing up and without uttering a word made it clear proceedings were about to begin. I had to laugh. The man looked so full of his own importance it was hard not to.

I won't bore you with the preamble that followed. It suffices to say that Bingham – who stood in the dock wearing a smart suit and looking as though butter wouldn't melt in her mouth – pleaded guilty and all that needed to be done was to await sentence but before the magistrates could do that, her lawyer as was customary on such occasions made a plea on her behalf for a non-custodial sentence and what a performance he gave.

He started off by saying his client was a fine upstanding citizen who had never received even a parking ticket before going on to talk about her charitable work and how any jail sentence would have a detrimental impact on her daughter who was only eleven-years-old and suffered from Down Syndrome. The best bit, however, was yet to come.

"The victim in this case," he said, "was not an upright pillar of community but a violent thug who uses rubber hatchets on those who stood in his way. Not my words, Your Honour, but the words of Mr Hatchet himself, or Hatchet Harry as he is better known to his peers and who on that now infamous show boasted that he regularly puts people in hospital who stood in his way, whether they deserved it or not A boast, Your Honour, that so enraged my client that for a moment she temporally lost control of her actions and before she knew it had slapped Mr Hatchet across the face. An act which she not only bitterly regrets but was completely out of character. Therefore, Your Honour, I hope you will look mercifully upon my client and give her a non-custodial sentence."

Then there was a brief pause, during which time the bitch in the dock began sobbing, no doubt to gain the sympathy of the court, before the pompous git running the show looked up and asked "if Mr Hatchet had anything to say?" My lawyer nodded his head and stood up before addressing the court respectfully, and he too gave a performance worthy of an Oscar I must admit.

Indeed, he began by saying that, "Mr Hatchet might not be an angel, but neither is he a criminal. He has no criminal record, has never been charged with a criminal offence, and like the defendant has no parking ticket." The last bit was a particular clever dig and I saw the defendant flinch when he said it. "Moreover," said my lawyer, "while my client may well have entered into fist fights with other young men who follow different football teams than his own, he has never have assaulted anybody in his life who did not assault him first."

I had to stifle a laugh when he said that.

"Additionally," he continued. "Mr Hatchet is not on trial here. He is the victim of a particularly violent attack perpetrated by the defendant and like everybody else here expects to see the defendant face the full justice of the law. I note the argument that mercy should be shown, but I understand that Your Honour only recently sent a black man to prison for slapping a stranger who had incurred his anger and do not believe Your Honour should treat the defendant differently because she is white and a well-known face. What sort of message would that send to the country, particularly with so many members of the journalist profession about?"

He pointed to the hordes of press officers around the court and I had to smile. The man was clever. By drawing attention to the press sat in the galleries he was saying to them, do you really want your name in the paper for sending a black man to prison for assaulting somebody but not a celebrity when she does the same thing? I mean, race relations may not have been as prevalent as they are today but it was 1979 and attitudes were changing, and more and more people were speaking against racism with the leader of the opposition under James Callaghan taking their lead.

It also appealed to the Anti Nazi League in court. Given their anti-racist stance, how could they possibly justify sending a black man to prison for one thing but not a white celebrity who did the same without being accused of racism themselves?

The magistrates too clearly appreciated the dilemma they were in because they kept casting anxious glances at the press, in between conferring with themselves about what action they should take against the defendant for her unwarranted assault. Eventually they came to a decision and when they did, most people in the court were absolutely gobsmacked including myself.

To cut the point, Bingham was sent to prison for twenty-eight days and the last thing I remember was seeing her being taken away by security guards with a look of pure astonishment on her face.

THE SECOND BLUE LETTER

As soon as I came out of the court I was accosted by journalist in all directions.

"Happy with the verdict, Harry?" cried one.

"Any word for our viewers, Harry?" cried another.

"What does it feel like knowing your attacker is in prison, Harry?" yelled a third.

It felt great and I said as much, but with all the media attention I was getting it really started to get to me, so I took myself off to St Ives for a fortnight with Biffo and the lads and had a whale of time.

Monica had said it was a great place to go surfing and though I had never tried it before, it was something I always wanted to do and I proved to be quite a natural at it. In fact, it was quite surprising really, because I had never shown any skill at sport, and yet here I was surfing the waves like a pro.

The only thing that did put a damper on my holiday was that the press somehow found out where I was and began hounding me for an interview. The whole thing was ridiculous. I would come out of the hotel and some slimy prat in a smart suit would say, "Any word for our readers, Harry?" or "are you enjoying your holiday in Cornwall?" or "are you relaxing after the court case, Harry?" At first it wasn't a problem and I took it in my stride but when it happens day in and day out it wears you down and eventually I had to say something.

"Listen guys," I said, trying to sound as polite as I could because I didn't want my name in the press for the wrong reasons, "I'll give you your interviews provided you leave me alone to enjoy the rest of my holiday afterwards."

They agreed to it much to my surprise and the next day, pictures of me appeared in all the major tabloids under headlines like, *Harry visits St Ives*, or *Harry visits Cornish coast*, or *Hatchet Harry rides the waves*, which was my personal favourite because underneath was a picture of me in my shorts, riding on a surfboard and having the time of my life.

I said, to Biffo, "Good picture that, don't you think?"

"Yeah, Harry," he said. "Real nice."

I give him a look. It wasn't what he said, it was the way he said it. So I said to him, "What the fuck's wrong with you?"

"Well, Harry," he said, shifting slightly on his feet. "You're staying at five star hotel, with first class food and service, and we're staying at a dingy bed and breakfast."

"So what?" I said, gaping at him in astonishment. "I'm paying for it. If you want to stay there all you have to do is get your wallet out and book in."

Again he shifted on his feet.

"Well, we can't, Harry, because we're not rich like you. So we was hoping…"

"What?" I snapped. "What were you hoping?"

"Well," he said, glancing down at his shoes to avoid eye contact. "We were hoping you would pay for us to stay there since you're earning bucket loads of cash."

I glared at him. "Pay for you. Do I look like a fucking mug to you?"

"No, no, Harry," he said, backtracking immediately. "I don't think you are a mug, trust me I don't."

I continued to stare at him angrily and eventually let it go, and got back to the business of enjoying myself and indeed had such a good time that when it came time to go home, I didn't want to go but nonetheless as our van pulled away from St Ives, I felt good, relaxed and completely chilled out.

My mum noticed the change right away because when I let myself into the house, she came out of the kitchen and said to me I looked like a changed man.

"Thanks," I said, putting my bag down. "Any post?"

"Post," my mum said with widening eyes. "Come upstairs and let me show you your post."

So she took me upstairs and threw open a door which opened in a room whereshe kept the hoover, ironing board and other bits and bobs. Now normally, there wasn't much in there, because my mother wasn't a hoarder by nature but today it was full of plastic bags and when I looked closer, I saw it was full of letters of all sizes.

"What the fuck is all this?" I said, turning to Mum in surprise.

"Fan mail, Harry," she said, with a slight twinkle in her eye. "You're quite a celebrity now and have your own fan club. Still, let me get you something to eat and then you can go through it."

So that's what I did and about an hour later, I was lying in my bed and going through the post and I must say it was an eye opener. Some were from girls saying what they would like to do to me, and sending me pictures of themselves, along with the phone numbers asking me if we could meet up so they could prove it. Some were from unnamed anti-fascist scum telling me I was trash and sooner or later they would do me, and some were from weirdos making all sorts of strange requests.

Then my mum knocked on the door with a mug of tea in her hand and placed it on the table by my side.

"Thanks," I said.

She then opened my suitcase, took out my dirty washing and paused at the door.

"Oh Harry, almost forgot. Somebody posted this through the letter box a couple of minutes ago. Didn't see who it was though. They had gone when I opened the door."

She handed me an envelope and closed the door behind her.

I could barely speak. It was a blue envelope and it reminded me of the last blue envelope I had received and when I tore it open I froze. For once again I was staring at a picture of me throwing the brick through the window of the car that killed that man on my first day at school. On the back were the words, *Meet me at Ludford Tower at one pm on August the fifth and come alone and bring ten thousand pounds with you. Oh, and don't try any funny business because if you do a copy of this photograph will be sent to the press, and the whole world will know what a cold-blooded murderer you are. And you are a cold-blooded murderer, aren't you, Hatchet Harry. A very cold-blooded murderer.*

LUDFORD TOWER

Within seconds, I was out the front door and scouring the street quicker than you could blink. There was nobody there other than a few old ladies and an old man with a dog and I yelled over to them, "Have you seen anybody pushing a letter through my letterbox?"

They stopped what they were doing and looked at me with puzzled expressions as though I had interrupted their tête a tête.

"Have you seen anybody shoving a letter through my letterbox?" I asked again, raising my voice even louder.

Again, they just stared at me blankly before conferring amongst themselves and then turning back to me. "No, love," one said. "We haven't seen anybody."

The old man hadn't either and I stormed back into the house in a fury.

"Anything wrong, Harry?" my mum said, as I closed the door behind me.

"Nothing I can't handle," I said, before dashing up to my room and locking the door behind me.

To say I was fuming was an understatement but worse, I was puzzled. I said when I got the first letter that the sender was very calculating and now I could add something further about them. They were patient – very patient. Well, they must have been, given it was practically a year since they had posted the first envelope, so they were not acting out of haste, were they? What's more, they must have guts and a hell of a lot of them because it took guts to shove it through my letterbox, it really did. Well, unless they had a death wish or something and I didn't for a moment think that was the case. No, what I suspected was the sender was both resourceful and patient and was nothing less than a blackmailer, and one who was out to fleece me for every penny I had. Well, there was no way they were going to get their hands on my money because I was going to kill them before they could, and when I say kill them I really did mean it so I accordingly made my plans.

The first thing I needed to do was to get my hands on a shotgun. That was not difficult as I knew that most farmers kept a shotgun on their property which they used to kill foxes or some other vermin, so one night I drove to an isolated farm and relieved the owner of his gun as he slept peacefully in his bed.

Secondly, I needed to get my hands on clothing that I could wear so I could discard them once I had killed whoever was blackmailing me and trying to fleece me of my hard earned cash. That too wasn't hard because all I did was drive to Wolverhampton wearing a suit, hat and glasses to hide my identity and bought a hooded tracksuit and trainers in cash. Sounds drastic I know, but if you paid by cash and not cheque there was nothing to connect you to the purchase of the clothing if the police came asking questions for whatever reason later.

And thirdly, I needed to drive up to Ludford Tower to check out the place. I wanted to see for myself where I was to meet my blackmailer so I could ascertain all the ways in and out of the place, and finding it was not easy as the place was in the middle of nowhere. On a number of occasions, I had to stop and ask people the directions and that was quite an experience.

"Ludford Tower," said an old man out walking his dog after I had asked him the way. "It's Ludford you want, is it?"

I assured him that it was.

"Well eh, let me see," he said, scratching his head.

One minute later, he was still scratching his head, so I put my foot down and sped off leaving him scratching his head even more.

"Ludford Tower," said a long-haired youth, after I pulled up outside a pub. "It's Ludford Tower you want?"

I nodded.

He turned to two girls he was with and winking at them said, "Should we tell him or not?"

One of the girls opened her mouth to speak but before she could reply I leaned out of the window and grabbed the little runt by the scruff of his neck and pulled his face close so it was only inches from mine.

"Listen, you little prick," I yelled, with such venom that he shook with fear. "Stop pissing me about and tell me how to get there now."

He gave me the information I wanted, and I sped off, leaving him and the girls looking on gobsmacked.

Ludford Tower, when I eventually found it, was in the middle of nowhere and a rather gloomy place at that. It was surrounded by a wooded forest and to get to it you had to drive up a dusty road which pulled into a large country yard where a number of old boarded up buildings lay in their decayed state as they had done for nearly a hundred years. I discovered later that the tower connected to an old pipe line which was connected to the local reservoir and back in the nineteenth century, the people who worked in the tower lived in these old unused buildings, and worked here day in and day out, seven days a week, fifty-two weeks a year.

Still, to hell with its history, the blackmailer had chosen his place well. Nobody could approach the tower without being seen and I quickly got to work. I hid the shot gun under the floorboards of one of the outer houses where nobody could find it and drove away. The blackmailer wanted paying and oh boy was I going to see he got paid. Not with money though, but with a blast to his lousy head from the shotgun I had just nicked.

MURDER

For the next few weeks I was on edge waiting for the day I would meet my blackmailer and put an end to his miserable life, not because the thought of killing somebody terrified me (it didn't), but I just wanted the whole thing over and done with so I could get on with the rest of my life and put the whole sorry saga behind me. So to keep busy and boost my bank balance even further I went on even more television shows and celebrity programmes. That was fun but then the day arrived when I was going to meet my blackmailer and oh boy, was I looking forward to meeting him. I was buzzing and couldn't keep still until at last the clock struck ten at night and I told my mum I had a headache and was going to bed and was not to be disturbed for any reason. Of course, I didn't have a headache and once I had locked the door behind me, and turned off the light, I climbed out of the window and made my way to the car, making sure nobody saw me as I did.

Thankfully, nobody did and a few minutes later, I was heading towards Ludford Tower and when I arrived, the place looked eerier than it did the last time I saw it, which was hardly surprising given it was now twenty past eleven at night and the place was in darkness. That didn't worry me as I parked my car behind one of the outer buildings and got out. What did worry me was that when I lifted the floorboards to get the shotgun out, it wasn't there. I couldn't believe it. It wasn't there and what's more, something else was and when I pulled it out and looked closer at it, I got the shock of my life, for

Hatchet Harry

what I was holding was a hatchet, a large, sharp as hell hatchet. I didn't have time to think any more about it because just then I heard a car pull up and I thought fuck it, I'll deal with this blackmailing scumbag using this.

I crept outside and in the darkness, saw two blurry figures getting out of a car before hearing one say in a cockney accent, "He's not here yet, so you stay here while I go for a piss."

He disappeared to answer the call of nature and when he did, I sneaked behind the other guy and as he turned around, I swung my hatchet with all my might and before he had time to gasp his head had flown off his shoulders and landed quite some distance away. I was shocked by that because I hadn't expected to behead him. I thought what the fuck, the little weasel's dead and that's all that matters because if he wasn't my actual blackmailer, then he was his bodyguard. His mate came running over then, saying he had heard a noise, so I swung my hatchet in his direction and that was it, I had taken his head off too.

I wasn't bothered about that either but I was anxious to see if they were carrying anything that could incriminate me, like a picture of me throwing a brick through the window of a car which had killed somebody when I was a kid, so I checked their pockets and car for any such evidence but there wasn't any. The only thing these niggers were carrying was heroin, and quite a large bag of it too. So I left the heroin with them in the hope the police would think it was a drugs deal gone wrong, and left.

The next day I was buzzing because I had dealt with my blackmailer and there was nothing to connect me with the crime. The only thing I could do now was to wait for the bodies to be found, and see what the police made of them, and that could take a while for they were killed in an out of way spot and it could take forever for somebody to stumble across them. So I took myself off to the pub to celebrate and what a great time I had. In fact, I had such a good time I bought everybody a round and when I woke up the following morning, I saw nothing on the news to lead me to suspect they had found the bodies or that there was a murder inquiry under way.

A few minutes later I heard somebody banging on the door, and after my mum opened it, I heard the sound of running feet on the stairs and a couple of police officers burst into my room and one said, "Harry Hatchet."

"Yeah," I replied.

"I'm Detective Sergeant Weston of Derby CID and I'm arresting you for the murders of Curtis Ambrose and Leroy Holden."

"Curtis Ambrose and Leroy Holden?" I yelled as I was put in handcuffs and led to a waiting police van. "Who the fuck are they?"

The police officer ignored me and I was taken down to the station and thrown into a police cell to await the arrival of my solicitor and when he turned up, I was taken to a room to be interviewed. All the time my mind had been racing overtime and I kept saying to myself, why are they arresting me, there is nothing to connect me to the crime, – unless those niggers had a copy of the picture and the police had found it and then I would have some serious explaining to do but as it happened they didn't. They had something worse. They had a video of me killing the two men and even though it had been taken in the dark, there was no doubt where I was, what I was doing, and what I was carrying because when I switched on the torch to search the bodies, the camera clearly showed me hovering over them with a hatchet in my hand.

I said to Weston, "Where the fuck did you get that?"

"In an envelope through the post," he replied with a smirk.

I won't go into the ins and outs of the discussion that followed but when Weston said he had no idea who had taken the video or for what reason, I believed him because I could see he meant it but I knew who had sent it though. It was the same joker who removed my shotgun and replaced it with the hatchet because who else could it have been, though how this joker knew I would be at Ludford Tower and why they would bother to switch weapons, I could not for the life of me guess. Still, with such damning evidence against me, I was hauled before magistrates on the charge of murder, and sent to prison to await trial.

The press had a field day when they heard, and pictures of me being carted away in a prison van appeared on the news and in the papers. That didn't bother me but what did was the fact that when I arrived at Birmingham Prison, one of the prison guards decided to dig me out and belittle me in front of the other prisoners.

"Now listen to me, Hatchett," he said, putting his face close to mine. "You might be a celebrity outside but in here, you're just a miserable little worm, got it?"

"Certainly," I said, before headbutting him so hard he hit the deck and was out for the count.

I didn't have time to jump up and down on his head and give him further cause to regret belittling me because about ten prison officers – or screws as they are called – surrounded me and dragged me to a cell where they closed the doors and began laying into me with their fists and boots.

These days, such things would rarely happen what with CCTV filming everything that goes on in a prison and social workers and other do-gooders monitoring prisoners' welfare but back in the 1970s, things were different and though I put up fierce resistance, I was fighting such overwhelming odds and it was only a matter of time before I hit the ground with my body and face black and blue all over. In fact, I was given such a kicking that I wound up in the prison hospital and spent the next two weeks recovering from my injuries. My mum kicked up a fuss when she heard of course, and it goes without saying the story made the papers but nothing came of it, the screws simply lied their way out of it and said I had been done over by a couple of inmates on my landing and that was that.

So for the next few months, I settled into prison life and that was an experience, I can tell you. There are two types of prisoners, those who give the orders and those who do their bidding. I don't do anybody's bidding so for the first few weeks, I was busy kicking, punching and knocking out any fellow con who fancied their chances and there was plenty of them, I can assure you, what with prison being full of hardmen, chancers, and outright psychopaths but they all wound up in the hospital wing and eventually I was recognised as being what cons refer to as the Daddy of the prison, or to put it another way, the person who runs the place while all the other cons do their bidding.

The day of my trial arrived and it seemed to me that the whole world had turned up to watch i, but the result was a foregone conclusion. Once the jury were shown the video it was obvious that it was me who had beheaded the two niggers and I was given a life sentence. I wasn't surprised by that but what did surprise me is that everybody thought I had killed them in a drugs deal gone wrong, given the victims were drug dealers who had been supplying drugs around Derby and elsewhere for years, or that they were killed because they were members of West Ham's Intercity Firm, but they weren't. In fact, I had no idea they were members of West Ham's firm until Weston told me that they were, though the fact they were was just an added bonus. I mean, who is going to miss a couple of West Ham Intercity goons? Certainly not me but all the same I couldn't tell anybody the real reason I had killed them was because they had a photo of me proving I had murdered someone in a car so instead I kept quiet and never said a word to anybody.

So back to prison I went and for the first few months everything went okay. My parents came to see me as did Monica, which always raised my spirits but then one day I snapped.

I was lying on my bed in my cell when this nigger called Leroy Sims, giving it the big I am, casually strolled in. I wasn't surprised to see him because he was new to the jail and had been putting it about that he was the new Daddy and he was going to put me in my place. He was also carrying a blade but it did him no good because the minute I saw him I smashed a hammer in his face which I had stolen from the prison workshop and he hit the deck quicker than a greyhound out of a trap.

I wasn't finished yet. It's an odd thing but ever since I had been arrested for murder, sales of merchandise bearing my face and name had gone through the roof and during my time inside, I had become a multi-millionaire. Indeed, Mr Levy, another person who came to see me on a regular basis said to me one day, "I know I shouldn't say this, Harry, but in your case crime really does pay."

Well, it might pay but I couldn't touch a damn penny of it while I was languishing inside. Worse, far worse was the fact that only that morning I had found out that the widow of one of the men I had killed were suing my estate for loss of earnings. I mean, her husband was nothing but a lousy drug dealer and there she was suing me to get her hands on my money. To say I was fuming would be an understatement and so when I saw him lying there unconscious, something in me flipped and before I knew it I had grabbed his knife and chopped off his head before tossing it out of my cell and onto the landing.

Naturally, I was charged with that murder too and hurled before the courts again, yet this time I wasn't sent back to prison. I was sent to Broadmoor, or the nuthouse as it is better known. For some reason the authorities decided that I was bark raving mad and too dangerous to be put back into the prison system so I was carted off to the nuthouse, kicking and screaming as I went.

Mind you, I wasn't kicking and screaming for long. It's an odd thing but being confined to Broadmoor is far better than being confined to prison. For one thing you can wear your own clothes and not those horrible drags you have to wear in prison, and for another you have your own cell, with a TV and record player, and you can come and go as you please. Even better, you had access to women. Unlike prison, the place was full of female nurses and female psychologists and there wasn't a day I wasn't in my cell shagging one of them. I'm not saying Broadmoor was perfect though, because it wasn't, and every now and again I did run into a bit of bother against some very well-known faces.

I was in the snooker room one day when in walked that prat, Roy Shaw. You know, the guy who wrote a book claiming he was the hardest guy in England and even mentioned his spell inside the nuthouse. Well, he walked in and demanded I leave because he wanted to play snooker on his own so I told him to piss off and go because I don't leave for anybody, and if he wanted to make something of it he could, but he would wind up in intensive care and I would take great pleasure in putting him there.

The little weasel came flying around the table and began laying into me with his fists and boots so I stood back and then ploughed into him and began battering him around the room. He was taken aback of course, and very soon on the defensive but I did not let up and eventually he wound up on the floor and out for the count, and he should count himself very lucky I did not have a knife or hatchet on me, because if I did I would have chopped off his head and left it on the snooker table for all to see.

Then there was that incident with that poof and so-called top gangster Ronnie Kray. I was in the library one day when he walked in wearing a pin-striped suit, with his hair gelled back and looking like he was the governor of the Bank of England. He glanced around and upon spotting me, he straightened his tie before coming over and saying in a cockney accent, "A word in your ear, son."

Now although I had never spoken to him before, or even seen him before for that matter, I knew who he was, because I had seen his picture in the papers and on television. He was one half of the Kray twins, and that he and his brother Reggie had terrorised London in the sixties, but that didn't bother me. What did bother me is when this poof came over, he leaned forward and said, "Touch my mate Roy Shaw again, and I'll do ya. Got it?"

"Certainly," I said, before punching him so hard in the face that he wheeled back over a chair and like Shaw, ended up flat out on the floor. I had to laugh. This guy was supposed to be a hardened criminal but the truth was he was a wimp and everything written about him was nothing more than hype, as I made clear when he regained consciousness.

"Listen, you little poof," I said, grabbing him by the scruff of his neck, "nobody rules the roost in here other than me, and if you think otherwise I'll take you somewhere quiet, and it will be me having a word in your ear, got it?"

Kray nodded as he shook with fear and that was it, this so-called feared gangster never gave me any trouble again and in fact, he was so terrified of me that he used to run the other way when he saw me coming, along with that other so-called hardman, Roy Shaw.

I was detained at Broadmoor indefinitely, which meant the authorities could keep me here for as long as they wished, and so the weeks became months and the months years, and before I knew it I was sixty years old and no longer the fit young man I once was.

My parents too were getting on and despite the fact they were in their eighties, they still manged to see me every month, unlike Biffo and the rest of the Derby Lunatic Fringe who I hadn't seen for years. Monica came to see me every month and I used to look forward to her visits especially as we used to chat about the good old days and the fun times we had had, but then one day she never turned up for her visit, and I learned later that she had died peacefully in her sleep the night before. I was devastated when I heard, and wanted to attend her funeral but the authorities wouldn't let me, they said that because she wasn't a close relative I wasn't entitled to attend.

So I mourned her death from the privacy of my cell and I had to admit her passing did bring a tear to my eye, the first time I had ever cried in my life and I used to lie there on my bed, sobbing away and thinking of the good times we had had. How she had always been there to cheer me up when I was down and how we used to sit there at the bar talking about nothing in particular. While I was inconsolable with grief, I got a letter from Monica's solicitors and when I opened it I got the shock of my life, for inside was a picture, the very same picture of me throwing a brick through the car window of that man I had killed, and I said to myself, "What the fuck is this? Why is Monica sending me this and how the fuck did she get her hands on it anyway?"

Well, the answer soon became clear when I read her letter because in it, Monica had written that the man in the car I had killed was her one and only true love who she had been seeing for quite some time. She said she had been on her way to meet him when she saw me lurking on the bridge and knew immediately that I was up to no good, so she had whipped out her camera just in time to take the picture of me tossing the brick that had killed him. She said she hadn't reported it to the police because the man was married with a kid and that would raise awkward questions about what he was doing there and who he was going to meet, so she said nothing and left it to fester in her and that would have been it if I had not walked into her life years later when she began running the pub. She said she knew who I was the moment she saw me because even though I was older and no longer a schoolboy, she still recognised me which is why she couldn't take her eyes off me when we first met, something I said at the time was odd.

That wasn't all. She said something in her made her snap when she saw me and she was determined to ensure I received my just desserts. She made her plans and though I won't go into the ins and outs of what that entailed, it basically meant that it was Monica who had written those letters threatening to expose me as a killer, it was Monica who had replaced the shotgun with a hatchet, and it was Monica who had filmed me killing those two niggers. She hadn't tricked me into killing them just to film me committing the act of murder so I would then be sent to prison and she would have her revenge on me for killing her boyfriend years earlier (important as it was), it was because they had recently gotten a friend of hers hooked on drugs and she wanted revenge on them too. So she had rung them up and, posing as a man, asked them to meet her at Ludford Tower at midnight so she could purchase a large amount of heroin from them.

I was livid when I read it and I showed the letter to the people who run Broadmoor, who then took it to the police but it did me no good. I was simply charged with the murder of Monica's lover I killed as a kid.

So here I am, now aged sixty-two, languishing in the nuthouse and all because of a murder I committed as a kid, and a woman who had spent years plotting her revenge. A strange end to a strange tale. Indeed, a strange end in the life of one of Britain's most notorious football hooligans, whose name will be remembered long after he has gone, and not just because of his exploits on the Derby terraces but also at grounds up and down the country.

Printed in Great Britain
by Amazon